Published in Great Britain by
L.R. Price Publications Ltd, 2021
27 Old Gloucester Street,
London, WC1N 3AX
www.lrpricepublications.com

Cover artwork by L.R. Price Publications Ltd
Copyright © 2021
Used under exclusive and unlimited licence by
L.R. Price Publications Ltd.

Story by Nigel Johns. Copyright © 2021

ISBN: 9781838339555

DEDICATION

Dedicated to all my grand and great grand children as long as you are over 18 when you read it.

DANIEL

Nigel Johns

1

DANIEL OPENED THE wicker gate beside the cattle grid, at the bottom of the farmhouse drive, and let Jessie, the eldest dog, through. The younger ones had learnt to make their way safely across, but Jessie had always refused to even try.

Following them down the lane, Daniel shrugged his shoulders and pulled together the zipper on his bodywarmer. He wasn't sure if, in fact, it was any colder today than the preceding few mornings, or if the chills were caused by the copious amounts of alcohol he had consumed the previous evening, and the fact that he had spent only three hours in his bed.

Still, the lads had made it a good night – particularly considering it would almost certainly be his last night of freedom for a long while. The judge had made it excessively clear that a lengthy custodial sentence would be ordered, when Daniel was to appear before him later that day for sentencing. And, by the judge's attitude toward him, Daniel expected the worst. He had been granted a week to get his affairs in order before sentencing, and today he would learn his fate.

Daniel's theory regarding the temperature was further supported when he chose to open the gate onto the bridle path, rather than vault it in his usual fashion. The dogs had already manoeuvred themselves over the stile and run on ahead, chasing the rabbits which hadn't already descended into their burrows, deep within the hedgerow. Daniel could hear one now, stamping its disgust, as he started up the swiftly steepening hill. Even in the first light of dawn, Daniel could make out the stand of trees about a mile distant, which were his destination. Silhouetted against the lightening sky, they appeared to mark the end of the world, with nothing beyond visible from that point.

Daniel reflected on the previous night, as he strode out on the rising ground. His teammates had organized a "by invitation" and "men only" send-off for him at the clubhouse. The latter stipulation had only been relaxed to include two club groupies, who appeared an hour or so into the evening, and immediately proceeded to place Daniel on a chair on the stage, with his arms tied behind his back. Then they started to strip.

With his back to the audience and the lights turned down low, they had teased him with sensuous, probing kisses and fleeting, light contact, their hands and nipples barely making contact with his knees and shoulders. They then unzipped his trousers and freed his swollen member, to stand proud and unseen by his teammates, each girl taking it in turns to further take advantage of his captive state, with their hands and mouths. Then, with only a very skimpy G-string left to cover her modesty, twice married and twice divorced – and still only twenty-four years old – Jennifer had pulled the skimpy piece of cloth which covered her modesty to one side and guided his throbbing member inside her, before riding him to oblivion.

Daniel had begged to be untied, but she had only laughed and leant back with her hands behind his neck, preventing him from reaching her hard, projecting nipples with his mouth, as she thrust in an ever-increasing tempo.

It had been left to Richard, his best friend and driver for the evening, to rescue him from his captive state, allowing Daniel to regain some modesty; even though he was in the shadows at the back of the stage, it was fairly obvious to all what had occurred. Obviously not fully satisfied, Daniel had then disappeared into the changing room where he saw the women make their exit.

Jennifer was still in the shower, but Grace was towelling herself with her back to him, one of her go-on-forever legs raised up on the bench, as she towelled it dry. Grace was older than Jennifer, probably touching thirty, but with a fabulous figure for a woman who had given birth to six children by a similar number of fathers.

Daniel quickly covered the short distance between them and, catching the end of the towel, he started to run it softly over a more intimate area. Grace certainly showed no objection to Daniel's wandering hands, throwing her head back to meet his kisses, and reaching behind her to once again free his manhood from his trousers. Daniel took her standing, with her hands against the wall. She joined him in climax, as he gratefully emptied his sac.

Sated, Daniel had rejoined his mates to rancorous applause, and slowly proceeded to become drunk – though not so drunk as to notice that both women disappeared for short periods of time on several occasions, throughout the rest of the evening; he guessed from other timely appearances that others had too enjoyed some pleasure from the two wanton strippers.

Richard had dropped him off about two a.m., and Daniel had crawled straight into his bed, without even bothering to shower off the body fluids which had left his nether regions messy.

Thinking back on it now, he felt ashamed – though at least he would be gone before Alice stripped his bed and washed his dirty clothes, scrutinizing each article before placing it in the washing machine; he would not have to see the knowing look in her eyes.

Daniel had now reached the section of the lane where it rose above the field to the left, for a few hundred yards, before the field lost its bowl shape and rose again steeply, to run at the same level. Crashing sounds indicated that the dogs had disturbed deer, resting in the rough of the bank which connected the two levels. Daniel watched as the three shadowy figures made their way through the maize, which was now taller than them, occasionally catching a glimpse of their bounding bodies as they ran to the top of the hill, before jumping the fence into a grazing field. After a brief glance behind them, the deer then carried on out of sight.

The dogs had run off much of their energy by now, and were starting to spend more time close to him. Jessie, the eldest, had already taken her place at his side. Daniel confided to her that it had probably been three young bucks who stayed together; he christened them "The Three Musketeers".

Daniel stopped and surveyed the scene to his left. It was now light enough to make out someone gathering up the few straggling cows who had not returned to the warm cubicles before milking, from a field beneath the wood. Early morning mists gave way to ghostly apparitions, with only the tops of trees. Occasional beasts were visible, lying so low amid the density of the mist that they might appear as bodiless beings, floating in the air. Today was one of those days, and Daniel watched as cows became whole beings again, emerging from the mist. Farther to his left, he could make out the outlines of a second dairy unit, and by the lights visible from nearby buildings, a similar scene would undoubtedly be transpiring there.

Daniel turned away and continued the climb, a slight moistening of his eyes betraying his emotional train of thought. The things he would miss were uncountable and irreplaceable – and the things which were undeniably free; one just need open one's eyes to see them. He muttered this aloud, bringing Jessie to nuzzle his hand. Daniel ruffled her head.

Jessie was now nearly nine years old, and the great grandmother of the two youngest of the four dogs. Jessie's own daughter had been shot by a poacher, just before her grandchildren had been born, which had convinced Daniel to keep two pups from each bitch. The two youngest were from different litters, and the two-year-old was to be bred on her next heat. Jessie was also the third generation from Daniel's twelfth birthday present: a cuddly, long-haired German shepherd he had named Elsie, who from day one had been his constant companion, and often dumb but always-knowing soulmate. Daniel knew she would pine more than the others for him, and he had already put some articles of clothing with his scent on them aside, to place in her basket in his bedroom, where she normally slept. He just hoped he would see her again. He had left instructions for keeping a pup from the next litter, but he knew there would not be that bond between them, which had been the norm with other generations.

Reaching the gateway, which led into the field with the stand of trees, Daniel whistled the dogs and climbed the stile beside the locked field gate. It was a shame, but some of the people now walking in the country had forgotten the old rule of shutting gates behind them, making it a necessity to lock them and provide a stile for easy access. A notice on the gate welcomed walkers to use the area for rest, shelter or simply to take in the spectacular views from all sides.

Daniel walked across to the enclosure surrounding the four ancient oaks, growing so close together that their branches were eternally entwined, giving extra strength against the winds which battered their exposed position. They had already shown their contempt for such winds by growing on top of a hillock. The sheer size of the trees overshadowed the ground beneath far too much for anything substantial to grow, but the rest of the enclosure had been planted with a wide variety of wildflowers and winter bulbs, providing colour and scent for most of the year.

Daniel had fallen for this area the first time he viewed the farm, and had already made plans for it before he had moved in. Two years after that, he built a bench around their circumference, carving both a memorial and a poem into it. Walking up the few natural-stone steps, he read the words carved into the backrest: *"In memory of Mum, Dad, Naomi and her friend, Liz."*

Reaching the top, he started to read the first verse of the poem he had written:

"Life is a road we all walk on.

For some the road is long, for others short,

for some the going's smooth, for others tough…"

Lily of the valley grew on imported soil around the trees and under the seats, its heads bowed as if in reverence of the place. Poppies and bright blue cornflowers were the most noticeable at this time of year, amongst the wildflowers growing below. Bluebells were his father's favourite, and abundant in the spring, while snowdrops and lily of the valley were those of his mother and Naomi.

Daniel bowed his head and stood in silent thought for several minutes, before turning around and sitting on the seat. He brushed off several immature acorns, which either the wind or birds had brought down, along with the first leaves to discolour and fall. He pondered at the fact that, of the thousands which fell each year, it was only the occasional one that escaped the attention of the squirrels and mice, and found an earthy enough place to grow. Any which did Daniel would remove, nurture for a year or so, before finding some spot on the estate to plant and propagate the next generation of these mighty trees.

His last thought before he had sat down was to wonder what his father would say to him now, if alive. Aloud, he spoke as if it were his father talking: "Well, Daniel, you've put yourself in the lions' den. Let's just hope they don't eat you up."

His voice once again brought Jessie to him. She rested her head upon his knee, her soft, sad, brown eyes looking deep into his. "You know something's up, old girl, don't you? Don't worry, I'll be back."

Daniel looked up and again slowly took in the view before him. From here, one could see for miles. Six-thousand acres of his land stretched before him, and he could clearly see the homes of both the reason and the cause of his predicament – although he was unsure of which was which. To their right, he could see the local villages and beyond, almost to Bridport.

He arose and slowly walked around the trees, their giant girth hiding the next scene, until one walked several yards. Below him, he could see the main road, which divided him directly from another estate closing in on three-thousand acres. Richard's home was on one of these farms, and if Daniel guessed correctly, his wife Jen would already be up and about, feeding the calves before herself and her family. A drop in the hills usually gave a panoramic sea view, but today a mist obscured that from him.

Looking farther to his left, over the hilly ground which ran all the way to the cliff's edge, far beyond his view, Daniel could see dots representing the grazing sheep and young stock which ran about this area, along with a herd of horses.

Daniel stood and shut his eyes, trying to drag an everlasting picture from his memory, until he could see it again in reality. He had come a long way since that tragic day. Sitting down again, he recalled how it had all begun…

2

JOSEPH, HIS FATHER, had been the youngest of sixteen, thirteen of them boys; twenty-four years separated oldest and youngest.

With the outbreak of the Second World War, all thirteen males had joined up, his father not even sixteen – only his father and Ben, the eldest, had returned home.

Joseph had a mathematical brain – quicker and more accurate in mental arithmetic than any calculator – and, with his eldest brother's contacts in the City, he soon acquired a position with a small merchant banker. Opportunities were numerous at that time, and Joseph, with his drive and desire to succeed, made the most of them. His employer was so impressed that he soon made Joseph a full partner. Ten months later he was dead. Having no direct kin, he had left it all to Joseph.

The business expanded rapidly under Joseph. But, being a country-bred lad, the hustle and bustle of London did not fill him with enthusiasm; he wanted only two things from life: a partner to share his life with and some peaceful surroundings, when not at work. His father had recently died, so he wanted to move back to Tilehurst, to be near his mother.

One Friday afternoon, after finishing work, Joseph caught a train to Reading, to visit for the weekend. After getting off the trolleybus in Tilehurst, he set off to walk the last half a mile to his grandmother's old house, where his mother now lived alone – except for an equally old and fragile friend, and two of her descendants, who acted as companions and did most of the household tasks.

He stopped to look at the properties advertised in the local estate agent's window, and one in particular caught his eye. Having made a note of the phone number, he called it the following morning and arranged a viewing for later that day. He arrived early and, as the place was empty, had a chance to look around before anyone else arrived. It was true to description, in as much as it definitely needed renovating, and the three acres of garden had seen more glamorous days, but it was full of potential.

Joseph was just trying to peer deeper into the gloomy depths, through French windows, when he heard the sound of someone walking up the gravel drive. Joseph was surprised to see a young woman, who introduced herself as Martha, the estate agent's daughter. She apologized for being late, even though she was actually right on time. Martha opened the door to show him around, and Joseph would tell her later that he had known from his first glimpse into the hall that he wanted to buy it.

Marble floors and pillars, with a winding staircase of ornate wood, to match the panelling on the walls, gave the appearance of grandeur, even though it was covered in dust throughout, and in need of a good clean and some fresh air. Walking through the rest of the house, Joseph could immediately see the potential, and later told Martha that he had felt a feeling of belonging.

The house had been empty for two years, since the previous owner had died, and solicitors had only just managed to locate the next of kin in America. They had not even wanted to see the place, issuing instructions for it to be sold, lock, stock and barrel. No real inventory had been done, but Joseph could see that there was plenty of stuff here which, if he didn't want it, would fetch fair money at auction.

With this in mind, he put in an offer about ten per cent below the asking price. He also managed to get Martha to accept an invitation to dinner that evening.

Over dinner, Martha confided that she felt pretty sure his offer would be accepted, but he would have to wait until the following week for confirmation, when her office could contact the next of kin.

Joseph was a keen sportsman; tennis, cricket, rowing and billiards were among his favourite leisure activities. There was already a tennis court there, although neglected, and plenty of large rooms, any of which could accommodate a full-size billiard table. There was a decent local cricket club, and the Thames was close by for his rowing. In all, ideal; all he had to do now was find himself a woman to share it with. And, if all went well, he considered he might have found the ideal candidate!

His offer for the property was accepted and, after pulling a few strings, the deal was closed quickly. By then, several dinner dates had transpired, and Martha seemed only too happy to oversee work being done to the house. Joseph asked her opinion on many matters, and always took her advice.

Five months after their first meeting, Joseph asked her if she would like to share the rest of her life with him, to which she readily agreed. A year to the day on which they had first met, they were married.

Ten months later, Daniel's oldest sister Ruth had been born. They had been keen to increase their family quickly, but with Martha's father suffering a stroke this was put on hold, as she was now expected to take control of the five estate agent offices the family had scattered around the Reading area and beyond. It was nearly another four years before Naomi was born, followed in under a year by his own birth.

Two years later, Martha's father suffered two strokes in quick succession, the second fatal. Her mother then succumbed to a fatal heart attack, shortly after leaving Martha in ownership of the family business.

Apparently, this was when Alice came into their lives. Daniel's earliest recollections of her were as a large woman with a huge bust, of about a similar age to his father. She was a kindly person, and Daniel had more memories of Alice from his childhood than of his own parents. Her maternal instinct – even for a confirmed spinster – left the children in need of nothing, with her unselfish love and canny sense of humour. She was strict to a point, but very fair, using her voice to control when they misbehaved – rather than a heavy hand, like their father. One look would be enough to stop them, because whatever she threatened, she delivered.

In all, their childhood was a happy one. When they grew too old to need a nanny, Alice's job description changed to that of a housekeeper.

Daniel and Naomi were very close, but Ruth had little time for them, which their elders always put down to the age difference. But, to Daniel and Naomi, it always appeared as if she resented them being born, and having to share their parents' affections.

Of his grandparents, Daniel could only remember his father's mother, who lived with an old friend and her war-widowed daughter, in a huge, rambling house still lit by gaslights, and still using bells to summon her maid or butler. She had always been bedridden, for as long as Daniel could remember, and he always felt in awe of her when he visited with his father. He was not allowed to call her "Gran", as that made her feel old; instead, he had to address her as "Auntie Pat", and endure her vice-like embraces, as she covered his face in bright-red lipstick and facial make-up, which she insisted on applying like plaster, to go with her bleached-blonde hair. Daniel was ten when, aged in her late nineties, she had passed away in her sleep.

Even though his family were very religious, and he attended chapel with them at least twice a week, he was considered too young to attend her funeral. Nor was he told at that time that she had left her estate to him.

Opposite their home was the entrance to a farm, and Daniel had loved to be taken for walks along the lane, from a very early age, always stopping to pet and talk to the animals which came over inquisitively at their approach. The elderly couple who owned the farm were always pleased to see children and, if they were there at the right time, they would be given a cup of hot milk in winter, straight from a cow, or icy cold milk in summer, straight from the cooler.

Daniel was about six years old when Mr. Parsons had allowed him to try his hand at hand milking: a sweet old cow called Darling who, if anyone pressed on her spine, would dip her back beyond belief, before crumpling onto the floor. After this, Daniel was totally smitten with farming. And, the older he got, the more time he wanted to spend there. Joseph, having been raised a country boy, and still possessing a great love of nature, was very understanding of Daniel's passion for country life, and did nothing to discourage him from it, other than to insist that his education came first.

Most Sundays, between chapel services, the whole family went for a long walk, as Daniel's father believed that the Sabbath should be a day of rest and relaxation. His parents' favourite walk took them through a beauty spot known locally as "Bluebell Woods" – an area of about four-hundred acres which, in spring, was a mass of bluebells. Silver birch was the dominant species of tree there, though a few beeches also remained, along with the odd fir, the rest of the mature trees having been felled during the war. Holly bushes and nut trees had also taken advantage of getting their fair share of sunlight and rainfall, having multiplied where once stood majestic oaks, elms and beeches. Daniel's parents had enjoyed many a ramble through these woods when courting, and Joseph, fearing that they would eventually be lost to building land, had persuaded the elderly owners to part with the woods for a paltry sum.

Daniel found schoolwork easy and, having passed his exams, found himself going off to grammar school. About this time, Daniel was horrified to hear from the Parsons that they were considering giving up the farm, as in order to keep up with current farming methods a large sum would need to be invested – at their age, they were not certain they wanted to do that. Daniel passed this information to his father who, unbeknown to him, had already had several meetings with the Parsons, and had in fact purchased the farm from them. He retained them to manage the place and oversee improvements. It was only on Daniel's twelfth birthday that he learned the truth, when his parents gave him the title deeds for the farm in his name, on the understanding that he continued his education and went to university.

Daniel, like his father, was a good sportsman, although they differed in their favoured choice of sports. Joseph was an excellent rower, tennis player and cricketer, while Daniel preferred athletics and, most of all, rugby, at which he really excelled, playing for his school and county, and attracting offers from several professional clubs as he grew older. Joseph was also an almost unbeatable billiard player, a room in the house having long now contained a full-size table. But this was one thing that Daniel had no interest in; although he would go rowing, play tennis or make up a cricket team with his father, the billiard room was somewhere he seldom even bothered to enter, let alone participate.

Joseph had never tried to manipulate his children into doing anything they didn't want to, but did encourage each to do their very best at whatever they chose, and to keep all things in perspective, with a view to the long term. To him, education had to come first, as it would provide their future security.

Naomi was also a keen sportswoman, making county teams in swimming, netball, hockey and athletics. Ruth, however, although she had obvious ability, was unwilling to put in any more effort than was necessary; she was content to simply tick over. Despite frequent arguments with her parents, she refused to continue her education, instead joining her mother's estate agency as a junior.

Here again, though, was a continual source of arguments with her parents, caused by her lack of commitment – often, she didn't even bother turning up for work. She appeared to have got into some bad company, and would disappear for the weekend without telling her parents, often not turning up again until the following Tuesday. Her mother continually warned her she would be dismissed and would have to provide her own living, if this behaviour continued.

Liz had been Naomi's friend, ever since primary school, but as they grew older, she began to earn herself something of a reputation as being a little too fond of the boys. Sure enough, these rumours reached Daniel's parents, and although they did not want to break up the deep friendship between the girls, they were keen to be careful that Liz did not become a bad influence on Naomi.

Naomi had not physically matured as quickly as Liz, though was beginning to catch up. Nevertheless, her interest in boys was far less than their interest in her. Daniel's friends had certainly begun to notice the changes in her, from a gangly but extremely beautiful girl into a desirable young woman, and were always keen to get an invite to his home. But Daniel preferred to spend his free time at the farm, rather than entertain friends who only seemed interested in trying to get either Naomi's or Liz's attention.

Liz's father was a bank manager and, although quite a wealthy man, his assets and income came nowhere near the combined value of the parents of his daughter's best friend. They too had become aware of their daughter's changes, and had admitted to Joseph that they wished they could afford to send Liz to a finishing school in Switzerland with Naomi – but, with one older and four younger children, they felt it unfair to drain their funds on one child. Naomi had also expressed her regrets that her friend would not be able to come. It was therefore arranged that they would take her there on a trip, as company for Naomi, to see if the girls liked what they saw there – if they did, then Daniel's parents would secretly help to pay the fees for Liz.

Coinciding with his parents' twentieth wedding anniversary, Joseph had arranged a few surprises for them whilst there, and had used the excuse of business to necessitate extending the length of time they needed to be in Switzerland; they would return two days into the start of the autumn term. Daniel was offered the chance to go with them, but preferred to stay at home and work on the farm, his declining answer meeting no objections.

Daniel's thoughts were brought back to the present for a few moments, when two jets on a low-flying exercise skimmed overhead, shattering the peace of the morning. His eyes lifted skyward – as they had so often before.

The noise abated, returning him to his memories of that terrible day, some thirteen years before…

It was the second day of the autumn term, and the day was going as normal.

During the first period after morning break, the deputy head breezed into the classroom and, after a brief word with the presiding master, called for Daniel to follow him to the headmaster's office. Daniel nearly had to run to keep up with him, his gown flowing in the draught his speed created. As they reached the cloisters, his steel heel inserts sounded more like a horse trotting than a human walking, as he spun sharply to his right, into the corridor past the bursar's office, and to the headmaster's office beyond.

On entering the office, Daniel was motioned to a chair. Two police officers – one male; one female – stood to his left, at the far side of the office. Daniel's first thoughts were that Ruth had come to some sort of harm, as she hadn't been seen for several days.

The headmaster, Mr. Simons, explained that the police officers would like a word with him. The words the young, female officer said to him would remain with him forever:

"I'm afraid we have some bad news for you. Your parents and

sister were on a flight which left Switzerland early this morning. Shortly after take-off, the plane developed engine problems and apparently failed to gain enough height to clear the mountains; it crashed.

"Rescuers have yet to reach the crash site but, from aerial views from other aircraft, it would appear that there is very little hope of finding any survivors.

"We are extremely sorry to bring you this news. We will take you home."

"Do you know the whereabouts of your elder sister?" the male officer enquired. "Your housekeeper said she hasn't seen her since last Friday evening?"

Numbly, Daniel shook his head.

The next half an hour or so seemed unreal, as he gathered his coat and bag from the locker room, and allowed himself to be driven home. Once there, Alice's hysterical sobbing and her nearly crushing him to death brought him sharply back to reality.

"Do Liz's parents know?" he had enquired of the officers. "When will we know for sure that no one survived?"

The officer replied that the airline would keep them informed, and took their leave shortly after.

Although himself in shock, Daniel knew that he had to take control of the situation, as Alice would not stop wailing hysterically. First, he called the doctor for her, before ringing his mother's office to pass on the tragic news, and tell them to send Ruth home immediately, should she appear – he didn't tell them of the tragedy.

He then rang his father's secretary in London, offering to keep them informed before anything hit the news or television. He picked up the phone book containing telephone numbers of friends and relatives, selecting those he felt were closest to his parents. He broke the news to them in concise, short messages, giving them very little chance to respond or question him further.

The doctor had now sedated Alice. Although he too had been a good friend of the family, Daniel dismissed him curtly, asking to be left alone.

A telephone call shortly afterward confirmed that there was no chance of anyone surviving the crash, and that someone from the airline would be in contact with further details.

In those few hours, Daniel had grown from a boy to a man.

3

HOWARD AUSTIN HAD been with Martha's firm since a young lad, having worked for her father straight from leaving school. He had missed out on any active service, because of his wasted leg from childhood polio, and he knew the estate agent business inside out. Daniel's mother promoted him to her assistant shortly after her father's second stroke, and delegated a lot of responsibility to him as the firm expanded.

A few minutes after five-thirty on that day, Howard knocked gently at the front door, hugging Daniel as he entered. Daniel was pleased to see him, not only because of his friendly nature, but also because he didn't know what he had to do next; he didn't even know if there were any bodies to bury! Howard immediately took over, compiling a list of people he would contact the next day. He then made some food, insisting that Daniel ate, before taking his leave, with the promise to be around the next day. It was Howard who answered the numerous phone calls, now that the press had details of those who had perished. He advised Daniel to leave the phone off the hook until morning.

When he had gone, Daniel let the dogs out, then poured himself a glass of his father's brandy. Sitting there, alone in the kitchen with only the dogs for company, the full reality of the day's events finally hit him, and he started to sob. Elsie placed her head on his lap, seeming to share his grief. She gently placed a paw on his thigh and nuzzled his hand, which he stroked her with almost unconsciously.

Because of his rambling talk to the dog, he didn't hear Ruth enter the house. As soon as he saw her and she spoke, he realized that she was under the influence of alcohol, and had no knowledge of what had happened. Between sobs, Daniel tried to bring her up to date, but she was so drunk that it did not appear to sink in, and she staggered off to bed without another word.

Daniel poured himself another brandy and followed her upstairs. He stopped and listened outside Alice's door; he could hear her snoring deeply. Obviously, whatever the doctor had given her had a lasting effect, for which, at that moment in time, Daniel was grateful.

He showered quickly and, having consumed the second glass of brandy, got into bed. He called Elsie from her usual spot at the bottom of his bed, to come and lie beside him, where he could cuddle her to him. It was like this that he eventually fell asleep.

Daniel rose from the bench and walked around the trees, to the other side. Reaching into the bodywarmer's pocket, he retrieved a pack of cigars left over from the previous night, and a lighter. Once he had taken the first draw, he sat down again.

The sun had now risen enough to send shafts of light through the still mainly verdant branches, to dance upon the ground below. The breeze softly rustled the leaves, the sun's rays making rainbow-coloured patterns on the dust particles drifting through them. The dogs had now settled, and were content to lie down and enjoy the warming sun. A pair of wood pigeons settled briefly, high above him, before their eagle eyes spotted either him or the dogs below, and took off with frantic, noisy wing beats. Around him, dry cows and in-calf heifers were beginning to stir. There was so much that Daniel would miss.

He loved living in this environment: the beauty of it; the smells, sights and sounds of the countryside; the changing seasons; and, the privilege to live as a free man within it. He loved to see if his breeding policies had worked, and if the heifers milked as well as he expected, or if a selected bull improved the conformation. Same with his dogs.

Jessie, his constant companion, was getting on now. He wondered if she would suffer and pine, and whether he would ever see her again. She had settled herself at his feet again, and Daniel bent down and ruffled her ears; a slight motion from her tail showed her acknowledgement of his action.

Daniel looked across the valley, to Richard and Jen's home.

Richard was his best friend, and it was to him that he was entrusting the management of his estate.

After the memorial service for his family, Daniel returned to school to take his O-levels.

Ruth had got even worse in her attendance at work, and Daniel instructed Howard to dismiss her. This did not seem to worry her, as she was spending her share of the inheritance, in the form of a large insurance payout. She had not even appeared offended to find that, for all intents and purposes, she had been cut out of the will, other than the insurance policy.

She still lived at home – that was, when she decided to return home – but, apart from vomiting all over her bedroom or bathroom on occasion, she caused no problems, even for Alice. Daniel hardly ever saw her at school, down at the farm or in meetings with Howard or Simon Banks – the latter of whom Daniel had now promoted to General Manager of his father's staff in London.

Daniel decided that he would prefer to go to agricultural college, rather than do his A-levels, as he had no interest in following any career other than agriculture.

It was at college that he first met Richard, then later Jen. Richard had come from a family where both parents worked in retail, in fairly unnoticed positions, but lived in a rural area. Richard was a bit of a boffin at school, and wanted to work as a land agent or nutritionist. He wore the thickest lens glasses that Daniel had ever seen, and because of this he kept himself to himself, lacking the confidence to mix in, while fully aware of his looks. They would probably have never become friends, had it not been for one of his fellow students – Philip Jewel – who came from an extremely rich farming family and, due to his ability to buy people, had gathered quite a group of hangers on. Daniel did not like Philip's attitude, and it was particularly his attitude toward Richard one evening that had brought

Daniel's distaste of him to a head.

Most of the students frequented the local village bars, for a few beers and games of pool, cards or darts. As most of the students were over eighteen on enrolment, their age was never questioned – luckily for Daniel. Daniel was enjoying a few hands of cards with some like-minded souls, when Richard came in. Daniel was not aware of what actually started the barracking, but he did not like hearing the jibes Philip was aiming toward Richard, while his cronies cackled at every cruel, cutting remark. Daniel warned Philip to back off, leave Richard alone and pick on someone who could defend themselves. Unsurprisingly, Philip then turned his abuse toward Daniel.

Without warning, Daniel sauntered over, directed some generic remark at Richard, then planted a sideways flung right hook to Philip's chin, felling him immediately. He then turned to Philip's cronies, but they seemed to have lost the desire to laugh anymore, or make any attempt to avenge their ringleader's fate.

Daniel took Richard under his wing from that day. A few weeks later, on a trip to the nearby city of Oxford, he paid for Philip to get new contact lenses, which changed his life. From that moment on, Richard hero-worshiped Daniel – to such an extent that it was necessary for Daniel to rebuke him on occasion.

With his newfound confidence, Richard started to mix more with the opposite sex – it was in doing so that he met Jen.

It was the classic love-at-first-sight scenario, and the two of them became inseparable. Jen was studying horticulture, in her second year. She was an attractive girl, but always seemed to dress in dull colours and shapeless, loose clothing. But, if one were to study her, it was all there to see. She oozed confidence and had a very determined attitude; she was definitely a good match for Richard.

Without the glasses, the bullies left Richard alone. Daniel had not only made the biggest of them look small, he later followed up with a warning that if Philip ever went near Richard again, he would get such a beating that no one would recognize him. Daniel was pretty sure he had wet himself, so terrified had he been when Daniel cornered him alone in a pub toilet. Now, though, he felt that Jen and her friends would have been a fair match for him, if he caused Richard any more problems.

Daniel had nearly finished his first year at college, when things took a dramatic turn for the worse.

He was given a message to phone Alice as soon as he could, on her sister's number. When he eventually got through to her, she was in tears. With Daniel away, Ruth had virtually taken over the house, and was inviting her friends for wild parties, leaving horrendous messes for Alice to clean up, as well as hurling abuse if she ever tried to bring some sort of order to what was going on. Ruth had been there for two days on this occasion, and even more people had been arriving for this current party. Alice could cope no longer, and went to stay with her sister in Newbury.

Daniel immediately left the college that evening and, by bus, train and foot, arrived at his home around midnight.

The house was ablaze with lights, cars were parked all over – including on the lawn – and loud music and laughter could be heard several hundred yards before he arrived there. The front door was open, and scores of drunk revellers were all over.

The music was coming from the main lounge, and Daniel made his way through the tipsy dancers and bodies sprawled about, to its source. He unplugged the power and ripped the plug off of the cable, to pre-emptively see off any rebellion.

A brief respite in the proceedings followed, as all eyes turned toward him, before some toffee-nosed spiv asked him what the hell he thought he was doing. Daniel replied that the party was over.

"All of you get out of my house, NOW!!!"

Having seen lights on the first floor, Daniel then bounded up the stairs, two at a time, throwing open doors as he went along the corridor. In nearly every room couples – and sometimes more – were engaged in sexual activity.

In his parents' old room he found Ruth and her latest lover, in similar state. He screamed at her to get out and never come back. When her fully naked lover took a swing at him, Daniel kicked him straight between the legs.

In the wing he shared with Naomi and two guest suites, he found his own door lock broken. Putting on the light, he saw two young women and one man performing some sort of three-way oral sex act. He didn't say a word, but just grabbed them one by one, throwing them out of the room, their clothes after them. He went looking for

Ruth again, but she seemed to have fled already.

When most were finally out of the house, Daniel started cleaning up the mess, ejecting any remaining drunk being he discovered, as he moved from room to room. He was still raging, particularly at the fact that rooms locked for privacy had been defiled – more so that they had broken into his room! It was in this mood that Daniel found some clean bedding, and sank exhausted onto his pillow, with Elsie beside him. She had been shut in a storeroom, but had soon given away her location upon hearing Daniel's voice. Her presence had been a great help in emptying the house.

Alice was reinstalled the next day, the locks changed and Ruth's belongings boxed and stacked in the garage. All traces of the drunken party had been removed, and the house thoroughly cleaned. A message had been sent to a friend of Ruth, giving his sister a week to pick up her belongings, or they would be donated to a charity shop. A van appeared two days later, and the entire amount loaded and gone within minutes.

Although Daniel heard of Ruth's whereabouts and activities from several sources, on numerous occasions, he had never seen her since that day, until she turned up at his trial.

She shouted nasty remarks at him as he entered the courthouse, and tried to get an audience with him through his barrister. With no response from himself, and her requests denied, she then took to sitting as close to the dock as possible, and muttering at a level that he could hear. He could feel her eyes cutting into him during proceedings, which annoyed him greatly. It was during one court session that he suddenly realized he needed to make a will – otherwise, if anything happened to him, as his next of kin she would inherit all that he had worked so hard for.

He remembered that she had a hatred of people picking their nose. Knowing that her eyes were trying to burn through him, and glancing around him to ensure that everyone else was intent on the witness being grilled by his barrister, he did just that; making it obvious that he had something on his finger, he placed it in his mouth. Daniel heard her muffled retching, but when he glanced in the direction where she had been sat, she was gone.

He would not be surprised to see her at the court today, for his sentencing, so that she could gloat. He put little weight on her desire to see him jailed not being fulfilled.

4

DANIEL LIT ANOTHER cigar and glanced at his watch, before turning his thoughts to Naomi and Liz.

Naomi and Daniel had always been close, and the fact that Alice spent a lot more time with them than their own parents when they were small meant that they had used each other to confide in – that had not changed as they got older, although they tended to follow their own gender pursuits more, and spend time with their own friends and pastimes.

Liz had always seemed to be around, and Daniel was aware of her transgressions long before they reached his parents' ears. He hadn't been too concerned with Liz's influence on Naomi, although he felt that she had definitely been instrumental in his sister starting to smoke. Daniel had seen her doing so on several occasions, though he wasn't sure if she was aware.

It was in the June before that fateful disaster that something occurred which changed things dramatically in his life, as well as his knowledge of the fairer sex.

Alice had an older sister, and had taken a few days off to be with her, as she recuperated after an operation. Daniel's parents had previously accepted an invitation to some friends' 25th wedding anniversary party in London and, rather than not go, they made Ruth promise to get home early and take responsibility for her siblings that night.

Daniel had come back from the farm around six p.m. and, after showering, he slipped an old pair of gym shorts on and ate the salad his mother had prepared for him, before leaving. The evening was still hot and the sun had still not sunk low enough for the heat to subside. Calling the dogs, he set off for a stroll around the gardens.

Rounding a tall privet hedge he could see Liz sat on a bench, while about forty feet to her right Naomi was partly hidden in the gap between a large garden shed and a hedgerow, puffing on a cigarette held in a long holder.

Daniel walked around the pond, with its large, ornate waterfall statue, between him and Liz. He would have just acknowledged the girls and gone on his way, leaving them to their own devices, had Liz not summoned him over to her. When he approached, she indicated for him to come closer and stand immediately in front of her; she then beckoned him closer still.

With him only about eighteen inches from her, she suddenly reached out and grabbed the waistband of his shorts, twisting it so that it was difficult to pull away. Daniel was also aware he was naked underneath, and pulling back from her would surely leave him exposed.

"You aren't going to run to Mummy and tell her Naomi's smoking, are you?" Liz demanded.

Naomi had been getting into a few arguments with her mother lately, and had probably made Liz aware of the things their mother had said – one of which was to ask why she couldn't be more like her brother.

Daniel shook his head; he would not drop Naomi into hot water. He could have done so already, as his mother had questioned him several times about her suspicions of Naomi smoking. He hadn't lied, but answered in such a way that nothing had been confirmed or denied, leaving it for his mother to find out the truth herself.

Liz tightened her grip and pulled him closer. "If you're a good boy, I will make it worth your while to stay shtum." As she said this, her free hand went up the leg of his shorts and started to caress his testicles, before taking his rising member in her hands. She started to masturbate him.

Daniel quickly became fully aroused; by God, was it good! Much better than doing it himself. Daniel glanced toward his sister, and could swear he saw her smirking as she pulled on her cigarette.

He could feel his member straining for release, and was thrilled when Liz pulled down his shorts and took his now rampant penis into her mouth. The feeling was sensational; his legs had gone like jelly, as his member strained to expand even further.

Daniel looked down and, grabbing the back of her head, as if to stop her pulling away, thrust his hand down the front of her revealing dress. To his surprise, he found that she was bra-less. He lifted a breast and, cupping it in his hand, he could feel the dampness where flesh had touched flesh and perspired in the heat. He took the swollen nipple in his fingers and twisted it from side to side.

Suddenly, it was too late; he couldn't stop: gripping her head harder, he exploded in her mouth. He need not worry, for she sucked every drop from him, her head frantically moving simultaneously with his jerking body. His legs buckled and he nearly collapsed to the ground. Liz gave it a few more sucks, before letting it slip from her mouth.

As she continued to tease it with her tongue, she flipped his shorts back over his nakedness and told him: "If you keep quiet, I might make it worth your while again."

Daniel showered again, his legs still like jelly. The moment he touched himself, it stiffened at the slightest touch.

What would he tell his friends? Girls were now an important part of their daily conversations and, even though Daniel did not believe half the tales that were told, he knew that he could well find himself subject to the same incredulity; he decided to stay quiet about the whole thing.

He'd had a few gropes and several French kisses, but this was the real thing. Every time he thought about it, it brought on an erection. Finally, having tossed and turned for several hours without getting off to sleep, he gave in to his needs and masturbated, reliving his earlier experience. Satisfied, for the present, he fell asleep.

Naomi was taking her exams, and consequently spent a lot of time at home, studying. So, with Daniel either at school or at the farm, they did not really see much of each other for the next two weeks. She had given him a wink or a knowing smile on occasion, over meals, but they never seemed to be alone to talk.

The last weekend before the term finished, Daniel's parents were away again, and Alice had taken a day off to visit an old friend; she would not be returning until early Sunday morning. Ruth hadn't returned from her date the previous evening, but she did phone to ask if they were agreeable to her staying away for the weekend.

On the Saturday morning when Daniel returned from the farm, he heard Liz and Naomi talking and giggling, as he passed Naomi's bedroom on the way to the bathroom. When he came out, all was quiet.

With a towel wrapped around himself, he made his way to his room. As he pushed open the door, he was surprised to find Naomi curled up on the chair by the window, and Liz sprawled out on his bed, in what his mother would have called an unladylike fashion. Her skirt had ridden up so high that there was little of her lower half left to the imagination. She rolled over so that she was now facing him and, moving her leg from side to side, offered him a view of her scantily covered crotch. "Have you still been a good boy?" she enquired.

Daniel's mother had been persistent lately, and asked him on several occasions about Naomi's smoking, which had annoyed him, because she only needed to look in the grass under Naomi's bedroom window to see the butts scattered, or watch out of the first-floor windows which overlooked the rear grounds, to see a plume of smoke rising above the bushes. He had warned Naomi of what he had seen, and also that she stunk of cigarettes; she was not to blame anyone but herself if she was caught. Daniel nodded his head to indicate that he had not said anything.

His mouth had gone dry, but his eyes were now glued to Liz's lower region, as she tantalizingly traced a finger up her inner thigh, before running it over her crotch.

"Are you sure?" she asked again, following her previous hand movements.

Daniel nodded again, his member already rampant, and pushing at the towel like Pinocchio's nose.

"Come here, then," she purred, reaching out to grab the protruding portion of the towel.

Daniel glanced at his sister, who was now grinning like the Cheshire Cat. Daniel didn't know if he liked her being present or not. One thing was for certain, though: his mother had good cause to be concerned about Liz's influence on her daughter!

The touch of Liz's hand made him lose any thoughts on the matter, and he lay down beside her, and eagerly met her lips and probing tongue as she pulled him to her. During the hasty unbuttoning of her dress and the rough removal of her knickers, they had changed the direction they lay in, so that Daniel was now facing his sister. He could not help but notice that her legs were now both raised, wide open, and her fingers deftly at work on herself, while she held her underwear aside with the other hand.

Liz pushed Daniel onto his back and climbed on top, taking him inside her before riding his shaft – slowly at first; almost teasingly, before taking its full length. Gradually, she increased the tempo and force of her thrusting hips. Daniel reached up and took her nipples between finger and thumb, pulling and twisting them, growing harder as her thrusting gathered momentum. In the background he could hear Naomi's moans of pleasure, as she neared her own climax. Daniel knew he was soon going to be there himself.

Letting go of one of Liz's nipples, he reached for her buttocks and pulled her tightly to him, before they exploded together, in what was the greatest sensation he had ever experienced in his life. His cries were so loud that Liz covered his mouth with her hand.

She slowly stopped the now gentle movements along his shaft, and her body stopped quivering with the multiple orgasms which wracked her body. She collapsed upon him, gently nibbling his neck, before finding his lips for a long and sensuous kiss. "That was pretty good for a first time, huh?"

Daniel replied: "Best thing that ever happened to me."

Liz kissed him again, then lay in his arms for a while, before saying: "I'll be back tonight; I have lots to teach you. Need to slow things down, so you last longer." Then she left the room, with the towel Daniel had on when he had entered.

He wasn't sure when Naomi had left the room, as he had not seen her go, but assumed it must have been during the moment his mind and body were in total oblivion.

Daniel went for another shower. He could hear the two girls chattering and giggling as he passed by Naomi's room. As he stood underneath the water, letting it wash away all the evidence of the act which had occurred so recently, he muttered: "God, no one will believe this."

When finished, he went and lay down for a short while. His body felt drained – but good. He certainly hoped she would return that night – he just wondered what she was going to teach him.

Daniel whistled as he walked up to the farm for the afternoon milking. He had never received any sex education from his father, but had seen the farm animals mating, as well as his dog, pet rabbits and birds. He did not find the act of actually copulating himself that much different – although, both he and Liz had seemed to enjoy it far more than the animals. He supposed they mated for the sole reason of getting pregnant... God, he hoped Liz had taken the necessary precautions! As much as he had enjoyed their liaison, he didn't want to become a father at fifteen, on his first attempt.

When Daniel returned from the farm for his tea, several more girls were there, and he was momentarily nervous. But no sniggering or knowing looks transpired, so Daniel surmised that nothing had been said.

He spent the following hour or so in the garden, alone with Elsie. He took her with him at about nine, to check the cows, as the Parsons had gone out for the evening. All being well, he returned home to wash the farm smells from his body and change into clean clothes. Hearing voices still about, he made sure that he dressed fully after his shower this time, only undressing when his door was shut.

He stayed awake for an hour or so. Even though his body – or, rather, his member – would respond every time his thoughts returned to that afternoon, tiredness at last overcame him; he could wait no longer and fell asleep.

Daniel was not sure what the time was when he was awoken, by someone gently sliding a naked body beside his, but it was dark. He would not realize until the morning that his curtains – which he normally left open, unless it was raining heavily, so that he could watch the moon and stars, and make shapes out of the clouds which drifted silently by – had been drawn before she woke him.

Daniel kissed and caressed the soft, lithe body, which seemed to fit so well against his, and those warm, wet lips, which apparently wanted to devour him. Liz's body slid down his, so that she could take him in her mouth.

After several minutes of pleasuring him, she moved up to kiss him again, before saying: "Your turn now."

She sat astride him, slowly bringing her womanhood closer to his mouth and probing tongue, before at last he could reach and taste her. She moved her body so that she was now almost sat on his face. She pinned his arms beside his head as she continued to gyrate her hips; she enjoyed the attention his tongue was giving her. She had leant back to catch his rampant member in her hand for a moment or two, allowing him to caress her body with a free hand, before she returned to pinning his hands down and pushing herself closer to him.

Daniel assumed it was her that again then took his penis in her hand... until he was aware that someone else was now lowering herself onto him. Daniel considered which of the girls he had seen downstairs that evening was now about to pleasure him, and herself.

In fact, he didn't care, so great was the sensation. Whoever it was was tighter than Liz; even though he could feel her juices flowing, she had struggled to take the full length – once she did, she started to ride him enthusiastically.

The presence of a second person appeared to increase the intensity of Liz's passion. Daniel tried again to see who it was, but she was hidden by Liz. All he saw of her was two hands, which cupped and caressed Liz's pert, swollen nipples, and slipped down between her legs, to compete with his tongue in pleasuring her now well lubricated, shaven vagina. On occasion, those fingers offered him the juices collected from their probing.

Liz came first, unsurprisingly, from the effect of the double attention she was receiving. This set off Daniel off; the unknown participant followed soon after. Liz stifled his cries this time, by grinding herself onto his face, so that he could hardly breathe.

He felt the third party disengage herself from him, as Liz slid backward and collapsed upon his chest.

"Was that good?" she asked.

"Unbelievable!" Daniel replied, as he pulled her down to him, to seek her mouth with his.

It was snuggled together like this that they fell asleep.

His rest was short-lived, however, before Liz woke him again, demanding that it was her turn now for complete fulfilment.

This time, it was a slow and tender build-up, with a crescendo finish. Then, still locked together, they fell asleep again.

At some stage, before his alarm went off to wake him for the morning milking, Liz had slipped from his arms and left his bed.

When Daniel returned for breakfast, Alice had returned. Her deliberate and unnecessary reference to doing the washing – on three occasions – made very clear to Daniel that when he went upstairs he would find his bedsheets changed; his dirty bedding obviously revealing evidence of the sexual encounters. Daniel tried to ignore the remarks, but was unable to meet Alice's eyes when she spoke to him, even about farm business. He had intended to change the bedding himself, before going milking, but had instead tried to grab a few extra minutes in bed, feeling the strain of his nocturnal exertions. In fact, he had ended up taking an extra half an hour, meaning that he hadn't even time for a cup of tea before running up to the farm. He had heard similar remarks before from Alice, like the times he had forgotten to take tissues to bed, and had either pulled out the side of the sheet or used a pillowcase to ejaculate in. For a woman and a spinster, she seemed all too well aware of his transgressions.

Alice informed him that Naomi had already breakfasted and had gone over to Liz's house, from where she would go on to chapel with her parents; it wasn't certain that their own parents would be home in time for morning service. She asked him if he had heard anything of Ruth. When he advised she would be home later, she just grunted and muttered something he couldn't hear.

Daniel had left a cow showing signs of going bad for calf, so as he was on his own at the farm that day, this would be a good enough excuse for his not attending, either. He had been thinking about it whilst milking that morning, and was truly glad that he was not a

Roman Catholic; he would have been spending a lot of time in the confessional of late, and even longer doing penance!

As it transpired, Daniel ended up missing evening worship, too, because the birth ended in a Caesarean section, which made him late in starting the afternoon milking. At least, though, both the cow and Charolais bull calf appeared fine.

Because of this, it was Monday morning before Daniel got a chance to speak alone with Naomi. After breakfast, she excused herself and went outside into the garden, no doubt to have a cigarette. With only three days left before the summer break, Naomi wanted to go into school, to say goodbye to her old friends who were leaving.

Together, they walked all the way down the drive before anyone spoke. There, Naomi skipped a few yards in front of him, before turning backward and saying, with a mischievous grin on her face: "Getting to be quite a stud, aren't we? Did you enjoy it?"

Daniel could feel the colour rise in his cheeks. "Well, yes, but I'm not sure I like the audience. Which of your friends was the second girl?"

Naomi refused to tell him, asking why it mattered, if he enjoyed it. Liz had given him a similar answer, when lying in his arms after the event.

"I would just like to know before I next see her again. Besides, I don't want her telling everyone."

They caught up with two other youngsters, making their way to catch the bus, which cut short the conversation. Once on the bus,

Daniel and Naomi parted company, each choosing to sit with their own friends. Daniel was well used to remarks about his sister's looks, and wondered if girls spent as much time discussing and eyeing up the opposite sex as he and his friends did.

In some ways, he wanted to boast of his exploits, but it seemed so far advanced of anything his friends had claimed, he didn't want to be ridiculed. Still, it was never far from his mind that morning, and he often had to rearrange the position of his penis, as it strained for release from his trousers.

The last period before lunch was Greek. Daniel sat at the rear of the classroom, beside a window through which the sun streamed. The discussion was about Homer's *The Odyssey*, and very boring. Daniel closed his eyes against the sun, and once more allowed his mind to drift back to Saturday night. Once again, he relived the whole thing.

He had just reached the part when both females were grinding themselves on different parts of his anatomy, and the second girl was interacting with Liz. He could feel the juice of one on his shaft, and taste that of the other; his hand was in his pocket, stroking the rampant being which sought relief.

Suddenly he remembered a detail – one he hadn't previously considered.

And, with that, Daniel leapt from his chair and ran toward the door. His attempt to make the nearest toilets was not to be; a stream of vomit hit the wall and floor before, he could even reach the door.

Daniel was now shaking, and sweat dripped from his head, as if in a fever. A teacher quickly ushered him to the sickbay, where he remained for the rest of the day. He was allowed to leave early, to miss the rush, after he confirmed that he felt well enough to do so.

When Daniel reached his stop, he alighted and made his way to the bench on the green, to wait for Naomi.

She saw him immediately as she got off the bus, and waved before walking toward him.

Daniel obviously looked ill, and Naomi's face changed to show concern. "What's up with you?" she enquired.

Daniel motioned for her to sit beside him. "How could you do it? Why, why? Why?! Don't you realize it's illegal – an imprisonable offence? Worse still, you could even be pregnant!"

Naomi's face dropped. "How did you find out? Did Liz tell you?"

Daniel shook his head. "Do you remember when you were playing with her breasts? I thought it was strange that it was so dark, and realized later that someone had drawn the curtains – but occasionally the moon would peep from behind the clouds, long enough to cast some light; it was during one of these moments that I clearly saw the hands. It didn't strike me at the time, I was so excited, but when I thought back I remembered seeing Grandmother's ring, which you wear when you're not at school."

"I'm sorry." Naomi lowered her head. "You needn't worry about me being pregnant: I've just started my period this afternoon."

Together they sat and an agreement was reached: Naomi would never do anything like it again, and not watch any further liaisons between him and Liz. Daniel was not sure he could even have any more to do with Liz, and told Naomi to lay off seeing her for a week or so. She assured him that she had plenty more friends who she could introduce to him; they would be more than willing to sleep with him if he desired.

It was nearly two weeks later that Liz walked up to the farm, alone, to where he was stacking bales on his own, whilst Mr. Parsons was milking. She apologized profusely, and took responsibility for what had occurred.

Daniel accepted, but immediately found himself looking at the low cut of her dress, and the seductive sight of her thighs, made deliberately obvious by the bottom two buttons having been left undone. He wanted her, and he took her roughly amongst the bales, there and then.

Liz was not the only one Daniel bedded that summer. When he told Liz, she made a pact with him: she would see no one else, if he would do the same.

Daniel often wondered what the outcome would have been, had Liz not been killed. One thing he was always glad about was that the secret shared between the three of them had died with them.

Unfortunately, Liz had given him an appetite for sex which did not alter as he grew older.

5

DANIEL ROSE TO stretch his legs, and left the compound for a short while to relieve his bladder. He then lit another cigar, sitting where he could see his home, and those which were either the reason or cause of his predicament. Daniel had met with all of them, within days of taking up residence on the estate.

After the upset with Ruth, Daniel did not return to college. He did not want to be an estate agent or work in finance and, although he attended meetings, he knew that he could rely on his staff to do their best – indeed, better than he was equipped to do, with his limited knowledge. This, coupled with his lack of desire, meant that he was better leaving things to those who did. Financially he was very well off, with inheritances and insurance payouts and, although he knew that he had the aptitude to do well at anything, farming was his chosen way of life.

Daniel had been enthralled by an article he read in a farming magazine, about the Holstein cattle in Canada and America: their larger size than the native British Friesian, their phenomenal food intakes and conversion to very high yields. He sought out more publications regarding them, and wrote to some of the top breeders in both countries. Several offered him employment after he finished college, and to educate him further. Alice was now safely reinstalled, and Daniel's request of one of his Canadian contacts, to go there immediately, had been met with a positive, welcoming response.

So, at the tender age of seventeen, Daniel found himself on a flight to Canada, nervous to say the least, on his way to what he hoped would be his future.

Daniel soon realized that in Canada he was going to learn a lot more than he ever would have done at college; the tutors lived in the Stone Age compared with what he learned during his thirty-month stay, and he was keen to try for himself.

Daniel had instructed Richard to keep an eye out for any suitable properties, and to forward their details with haste. It was the estate in Dorset which caught Richard's eye, and it proved an excellent choice.

Vacant possession was on Michaelmas Day, but there were options to buy, lock, stock and barrel, which would at least give the estate an income, whilst Daniel implemented changes. Daniel gave Richard instructions to make an offer for the estate, and engage a well-regarded firm of auctioneers to represent him in the valuation, but any substandard stock or equipment he wanted rejected prior.

Daniel immediately enquired about exporting and importing stock from and to England and, given a green light, purchased selected young heifers and heifer calves to start his own herd of Holsteins in the U.K., as well as semen and two young bulls from the best families he could find. The executors of the estate were also agreeable to providing quarantine facilities for any animals sent over before that date, so Daniel immediately arranged shipment for eighty animals, and his present employer would continue to source stock once he returned home.

It was while looking over a bunch of heifers – which had completed their quarantine period and been turned out to graze, before he arrived back in the U.K. – that he first met his neighbour, Tony. The field the heifers were grazing was on the boundary of the two farms and, as Daniel reached the gate, a truck pulled up on the verge. Tony's opening remarks, accompanied by chuckling, were to play a major part in their future relationship: "What's that you been looking over? Because they look like a bunch of ostrich-legged hat-racks to me." At that time, neither was aware of who the other was, and it was obvious that Tony was shocked to find out the youth stood before him was in fact his new neighbour, rather than a farmworker.

Tony, it transpired, was a very keen British Friesian man, who had quite a reputation as a show man, breeder and milk producer. His views on the bigger framed, bonier, leggier and much taller and capacious Holsteins was often unprintable, and the leg-pulling between them would become part and parcel of their relationship.

That first meeting included an invitation for Sunday lunch and, as Alice was still packing up his old home, Daniel accepted gratefully.

Tony's farm was only about nine-hundred acres. A smaller property of eighty acres had at some time in the distant past belonged to the estate, but had been sold off to satisfy the beneficiary of a will, a couple of generations ago.

Daniel showered after the morning chores were finished, picked some flowers from the garden and selected a bottle each of red and white wine, from those left by the outgoing owners, that he might enjoy a housewarming, before he set off for the few minutes' drive to Tony's.

Daniel immediately noted the tidy, well-kept appearance of the land and buildings, as he passed on the approach road to the farmhouse. The milking herd was grazing adjacent to the road and, although not the type of cattle that Daniel favoured, he had to admit that this guy knew his onions.

Tony himself answered the door and ushered him through, into a large lounge, where two Jack Russells jumped up his legs, seeking attention. Tony's little boy was just about to turn out a box of toys and, on seeing him, picked up a tractor, which he brought over to show to Daniel. A baby girl was happily bouncing in a swing, attached to the doorframe. Tony called to his wife, to come and say hello.

Daniel was surprised by the woman who answered his call; she looked a lot younger than Tony, and to say that she was striking would be a definite understatement. Introducing herself as Tina, she graciously accepted the flowers and wine, giving him a peck on the cheek, jointly as a welcome and a thank you.

Over the delicious, three-course meal she had prepared, Daniel ascertained that Tony was ten years older than Tina, and they had been married for five years. She had been eighteen when they married, making her twenty-three now – three years older than Daniel. Sam, their eldest, was pushing four, and Victoria fifteen months. Tony could not resist rubbing it in when Daniel complimented the beef, that it was home-produced from a Friesian/Hereford heifer, with a definite emphasis on the Friesian. There followed a lengthy but light-hearted debate on the attributes of both breeds, with Tony eventually winning the argument by stating that, up until now, it was all hearsay; none of Daniel's imported stock had yet to produce a litre of milk.

Leaving Tina to clear away the dinner dishes, Tony showed Daniel around the farm and stock. Tony was obviously proud of his achievements and, in all fairness, Daniel could only compliment him. Tony had inherited the farm from his grandfather, his mother having been an only daughter and married to a mainly arable farmer; Tony was delighted to continue the herd his grandfather had nurtured. Several of his bulls had made the grade and stood at A.I. centres throughout the U.K., their semen producing thousands of calves each year – a fact which Tony was openly proud of.

The tour over, they then returned to the house. Although Tina suggested that he stay for tea, Daniel needed to get back, as he was doing the milking on one of his dairies that afternoon.

Still, the day had sowed the seeds of a friendship which bonded them together for the next eight years. Although Daniel had his own ideas, he was often glad to call on the experience of his neighbour.

Some of Daniel's methods and cropping rotations certainly caused a few raised eyebrows – especially when he grew so much maize, fodder beet and Lucerne. A lot of his grass was only in highly productive, short-term leys, but the benefits were enormous, including the quality of feed going into his cattle's mouths, as well as finishing his beef cattle earlier and improving the lambing percentage.

At first, Daniel had only enough imported stock for the formation of one herd but, over the years, this expanded to four, whose foundations had started with these cattle or with a few new ones he brought in every year, from top cow families. The other two herds were the progeny of the best of the original herds, taken on when he moved in, except that they had all been crossed with pure Holstein bulls, and were now nearly pure themselves.

Daniel also purchased some animals in the first couple of years, at Tony's draft sales, from milkier cows with finer bone, and proved that even these would produce more milk under his regime. This fact was not missed by Tony. It was a semen rep which let on that Tony had in fact purchased some imported Holstein semen.

Daniel could see that Tony was begrudgingly starting to admire the attributes of his cattle and, armed with the knowledge that Tony had purchased the semen, Daniel led one of the almost-white twin heifers up Tony's drive early one Christmas morning, where he tied it to his porch with a sign around its neck, reading: *"Happy Christmas."* Being so white, Daniel knew that he could monitor it easily, even from a distance.

Breed of cattle wasn't the only thing the two them differed on: Tony was a keen footballer, playing for the village team, while

Daniel joined the local rugby club. Tony referred to rugby players as "thugs", whilst Daniel referred to footballers as "wimps" – even so, though, they would often attend each other's social evenings.

Tina tried to get Daniel paired off with some of her single friends. Unless Daniel categorically stated that he had a date, nearly every time they went out together, or he accepted an invite to dinner, a friend of Tina's would miraculously appear to make up the foursome, or conveniently just be passing through.

He did find some of her friends attractive, but either they started talking of marriage on the second date, or he simply had little in common with them. Daniel realized that, unless he got his act together, he would either end up with some second-hand rose, or just get married for the wrong reason. He liked the women who hung around the rugby club, as it was easy to find one to satisfy his immediate needs; as far as women were concerned, his social life seemed to revolve around the rugby club.

Both Tony and Daniel found Tina's attempts at matchmaking funny, but when alone Tony implied more seriously that he ought to find himself a wife. "Who's going to do your cooking and washing when Alice retires?" was a common quip.

Daniel told Tina that if she could clone herself, he would get married in an instant! As far as he could see, she was the ideal partner in every respect – Tony had also hinted, on more than one occasion, that she was good in bed! "A lady by day and a whore by night," he had once said, when more than slightly inebriated.

In fact, Daniel envied the relationship his friends had, and he enjoyed being around their children. He even accepted the responsibility of being a godparent to their third: another boy, named Timmy.

It was obvious to both Daniel and Tina that there was some chemistry between them, but both had not allowed it to grow – all except for one occasion: a New Year's Eve when, struggling to find a babysitter, Tony and Tina decided to host a party themselves. Alice and Daniel had both been invited and, during the course of the evening, Daniel found himself dancing with Tina on several occasions – one of them a slow, smoochy number, during which she had been very close, and Daniel had to resist the impulse to hold her closer. Later that night, shortly after the bells had struck, Daniel found himself alone with her in the kitchen, when she came to wish him the best for the new year. The kiss had developed from a peck on the lips to a full-on French kiss, before both immediately realized they had gone too far and broke away. Tina apologized the next day, taking the blame and putting it down to the drink. As no one was any the wiser, it was not mentioned again – although, for a while, their friendship was cautious.

The only other occasion when things had been a little awkward was one evening at the rugby club. A local child with a rare disease needed treatment in America, and it was suggested that the club hold a slave auction, with the slaves donating twenty-four hours of their time to the highest bidder, to raise funds for the youngster. Daniel agreed to be one of the slaves and, like most of his teammates, decided to dress as one. It was late September, and Daniel was already well tanned from a summer of working outdoors. Alice made him an outfit akin to those of the gladiator era, and with the addition of some oil on his muscular body and a chain or two, he really looked the part. The auction was scheduled to start at 7.30 p.m., with a parade of the slaves beforehand, where prospective bidders could question their shortlist on suitability for the work they intended to allocate, should they successfully bid for them. As most were fairly local lads, their capabilities were already known to most, but the charade of parading them, cracking a whip and generally stirring up the audience, by making the slaves flex their muscles, open their mouths, or some such role-play, was acted out with goodwill. Daniel had his toga lifted twice, discreetly, and occasionally a hand would reach for his manhood, cupped in a leather thong – firstly by one of the three more "suggestive" women in the village, who hung around together, and then by the old postmistress, who had seen the previous encroachment and followed suit for a laugh.

The auctioneer started his build-up from the rostrum, during which he declared that he would only accept suitable bids, and that any bids deemed unsuitable would be ignored. Daniel was lot eight, and from the wings was able to discreetly watch the first lots being sold. John Crow, the club president, was enjoying his time in the limelight as ringmaster, cracking jokes and the bullwhip, as he paraded each slave for auction.

Roger Dean, a fellow teammate and carpenter by trade, was lot one. He was certainly a useful man to have for the day, and raised ninety-two pounds, from a couple renovating a farmhouse just outside the village, who were already employing his services. Lot two was Tim Burgess, again a teammate, whose normal income came from driving a digger. He was purchased by "Digger" Jones, so-called because he kept the local graveyards in order, as well as digging new graves. He showed his delight at having secured Tim's services, by telling him that he would be fulfilling advance orders, by getting off his arse and digging a few holes by hand. His laughter was nearly drowned by the auctioneer's introduction for the next lot.

When came Daniel's time to be paraded on stage, Roger still held the highest price so far, by two pounds. Daniel was started at ten pounds by another local farmer, who shouted that if he got him he would have to milk some real cows, referring to the herd of Jerseys he owned. He was soon outbid by another farmer, whose only stock was pigs; he had retorted that Daniel would know what real shit smelt like, if he purchased him. The two of them contested the bidding to fifty pounds, when Julie Stephens and her two friends, Jennifer and Grace, suddenly came in, bidding fifty-two. The two initial bidders came back with a few more bids, until Julie stepped up the bidding with a five-pound raise to seventy-five.

With the hammer poised to fall, Tina suddenly came in and bid eighty pounds, quickly followed by alternate bids, up to one hundred. Tony tried to persuade Tina to stop, but the bidding had continued to one-twenty, at which stage Tony pulled Tina back down into her seat. Obviously put out, he told her emphatically to stop and let the girls have him. This she had reluctantly done, complaining that the three girls had made it perfectly clear they only wanted him for his body. Tony retorted that at least he would enjoy it more than the things other bidders would have set him to do.

An argument had developed, with accusations being thrown – to which Daniel was privy, as he was now seated on the next table to Tony and Tina, along with his three purchasers. The women were making it abundantly clear what he would be expected to do – or, rather, what *they* were going to do with him. Tina ended up leaving in a huff, and Tony soon after, giving Daniel a squeeze on the shoulder as he passed.

Daniel remembered it being a long night. He could not handle three women at once, but tried to make sure that each received a similar amount of attention. After the initial onslaught, some sort of rota was agreed until, luckily for Daniel, the alcohol took its effect, and he managed to get a few hours of sleep. One of the girls had fallen asleep holding his cock in one hand and her mouth agape; she had passed out in a drunken stupor trying to give him oral sex. Daniel had been glad to feel his member slacken and withdraw from her mouth.

It was nearly ten before any of them woke and joined him in the lounge, where he had spent the last four hours alone. Julie was the first to sober up, and had the sense to suggest that it may be better to have individual sessions from now on. At least there were respites for meals.

Daniel had no regrets, even though he knew that a lot of the villagers would be giving him dirty looks, once the story got around.

He just hoped the girls would not add fuel to the fire. It had been agreed that all slaves were to be returned to the rugby club for a nine o'clock roll call. But, to his dismay, someone had tipped off a reporter from the local rag, who not only brought along a photographer – who clicked away as if his life depended on it – but seemed determined to get a good story. Although Daniel refused to get drawn into giving any details away, there were plenty there who were happy to spill the beans. Daniel was glad that neither Tony nor Tina had chosen to come back for the sign-off, but annoyed the following Thursday to find his picture on the front page, above a story which wasn't too far from the truth. The fact that it had been for a good cause had also come to the notice of the nationals, and it was a case of hide and seek for the next few days, as Daniel sought to escape their attention. The only good thing to come out of it was that the donations made to the fund meant it had all been worthwhile.

Daniel chatted with Tony the following day, and they had a good laugh about it, but it was a week before Daniel saw Tina again. Tony told Daniel that he had accused Tina of fancying him, among other things, and this made things very awkward, even though she was unaware that Tony had spoken to Daniel. Still, eventually – apart from the odd snide remark – things returned to normal.

Tina continued trying to pair him off with some nice girl or other but, as before, they always seemed to fall into either one of the two categories: either they started talking about marriage and kids on the second date, or they made it quite clear that there would be no sexual activity until a ring was on their finger. Daniel was sure that the majority of the second group were definitely not virgins – if they were, at their age, it would not be lube they required, but rust remover.

He was sure that all had been primed by Tina, in some way. He told her again one day, over dinner, that the best thing she could do was get herself cloned, as he had previously suggested, or forget the whole idea. It was not that he fancied Tina, but in her he could see everything that made a good wife and mother. She just had something about her, more than looks. In some ways, she reminded Daniel of Naomi, in a lot of her mannerisms.

He was generally happy with his life, but secretly admitted to himself that he really needed to find a wife. But, with his reputation, he had to admit that this was not an easy task – after the slave auction it would be even harder.

6

DANIEL'S THOUGHTS TURNED to the other part of the puzzle his life had become: the Tobins.

By all accounts, their farm had belonged to Mrs. Tobin's parents, and they had not been very impressed by her choice of husband. The farm had always been well run, but once her parents had left this world, it gradually deteriorated. She had produced her sixth child, with no more than a year between most of them, two years before Daniel had moved in. Looking after her brood and trying to manage the farm, while her useless husband Jimmy drank or gambled away any profits on a daily basis, had proved too much for her, and the place had gradually become a graveyard for broken machinery; the fields produced more weeds than fodder. Jimmy was the kind of person who would cut his hay grass the day before it rained, after ten days of glorious weather, or wait until his silage grass was seeded and of poor quality. The stock was poor quality as well, and the ministry vet was often seen there, checking them over, so frequent had been the reports of neglect.

Daniel had always found her a pleasant woman, and he knew that she did her best, but the two eldest children were both boys, and destined to become a likeness of their father. Daniel offered them both work as they grew older, both as full-time and seasonal workers, but only one turned up at all, and he had disappeared by dinnertime.

Tommy, the eldest, had a miraculous escape when, riding pillion on a stolen motorcycle with his cousin Cam, he had been thrown off into a pond when they had crashed, whilst being chased by several police vehicles. His cousin had been killed instantly and, according to the local gossip, was not to be missed.

The third born, a girl named Sophie, was like her mother: quiet, polite and studious, and often seen trying to do men's work with her mother. Rumour had it that Mrs. Tobin had been a smart woman in her youth, and observing Sophie it was obvious that she would attract plenty of looks as she matured. Looking closely at the two of them, as Daniel chatted to them one day, beneath the lines and frowning on the older woman's face, the resemblance in their features could be seen.

Mrs. Tobin met an unexpected end about three years ago. She was found collapsed in the yard by the postman, and unfortunately found to be in the later stages of cervical cancer; she died a few weeks later. Sophie, being the oldest girl, tried to take her mother's place, cooking and cleaning for her father, two older brothers and younger sister and brothers.

Not long after the funeral, the two youngest lads had, according to village gossip, been sent to live with their mother's relations in Wiltshire, but – again, according to gossip – although only fourteen, Sophie had refused to let her younger sister go as well. Sophie would take her to school and would wait in the village for her to return on the school bus, before walking home together.

Daniel, among others, would try and help, dropping in the odd bag of potatoes, basket of veg, home-baked bread and cakes, meat or bags of chicken corn. He would also place a few pounds in with his offering, and Alice would pick her and her sister up some clothes or shoes.

About a year after, Sophie and her sister had been walking past the village shop, when Alice almost bumped into them as she exited. Being a hot day, she gave both girls some loose change to go in and get themselves a lolly, sweets and a drink. Sophie sent her sister in, but put Alice's offering for her into her pocket. When Alice commented on this, she said that she saved all she could, as she didn't know how long she could stay here, but she wouldn't comment further.

Alice passed this on casually over dinner that evening. Daniel told her to tell Sophie that he would find somewhere for her and her sister to live, and find her some work. But the girls had not been seen and, despite a lot of local rumours, Daniel believed her father's claim that the girls had disappeared, and he didn't have a clue where they were. The local constabulary made a few tentative efforts to find them, and put them on a national register for missing persons, but after a few weeks the local jungle drums had gone quiet.

The two older lads – especially Tommy – seemed to do less and less, except skulk around the area making a nuisance of themselves or committing some minor felony. They showed little brain, and were nearly always caught immediately. Among some of their more stupid acts were to steal an erected tent from a local campsite and erect it in the garden at home, and to steal someone's dog, which was tied up outside a shop in Bridport, then try to sell it in one of the local pubs where, unfortunately for them, the owner's husband was taking a drink after work. The local girls all gave them a wide berth – especially after Tommy had been lucky to avoid prosecution for attempted rape. The village bobby had told Daniel that his superiors considered the pair of them half-baked, probably from the thick ears their father had inflicted on them in a drunken stupor. They were fed up with the light punishments handed down by the local beaks, on the boys' regular appearances before them, and considered it a waste of their time altogether charging them, because they then had to chase them for non- payment of fines.

As for Tobin Senior, he was no better, having spent several spells incarcerated for various misdemeanours – mainly drink- or theft-related – and would never change. He was serving twelve months for assault when the event happened, but it was Tommy who was the cause of Daniel's predicament on this day.

In reality, it had started about two years ago, with Tony's own devastating news that he had testicular cancer, and it had spread. Initially he hadn't even told Tina, but as his health deteriorated he did so, with Daniel present. For several months, Tony's condition was kept within a tight circle, but eventually it slipped out and became common knowledge.

It also became knowledge that Tony could no longer make love to Tina. Daniel had been aware of it for some time, and his friend informed him that he had suggested she seek Daniel out for sexual satisfaction. Tina had a high sex drive, according to Tony, but she had been horrified at his suggestion, and it was never mentioned again.

Both Tony and Tina had used Daniel as their confidante, sharing their fears and problems with him. But, in late May, a year ago, something occurred which would change Daniel's life considerably.

Spring had been early that year, and the continued good weather meant that the first cut of silage was also. Tony's health was deteriorating visibly, and Tina was struggling to come to terms with her impending loss.

Tina was a member of the local women's craft guild, who met fortnightly in the village hall. She had rung and asked Daniel to call in at some stage during that Thursday evening, to check on Tony and the children. Then, being a fine evening, she decided to walk the mile or so to the meeting. She was gone when Daniel arrived and, with the children asleep and Tony dozing in his chair, Daniel left a note for Tina then went home, a little before ten.

Daniel could sense that something was wrong, speaking to Tina the following morning, when he phoned to enquire how Tony was. Puzzled by Tina's attitude and her continued reluctance to talk, Daniel went over to see her that evening. It was obvious that Tina had been crying, yet Tony was himself in remarkably good spirits for a dying man, and did not give any indication he was aware of Tina's state of mind. Tina also seemed to actively avoid any situation where Daniel might get a chance to question her, although he did manage to ascertain that it was not Tony's health or anything he had done that was causing her distress.

He was even more concerned when he twice saw her wiping tears from her eyes, as she sat in a chair slightly behind them, rather than in her usual place beside Tony. At one point, she even suggested that Daniel leave, as Tony was tired.

It took nearly a week for Daniel to catch her away from the house and in private, when he demanded that she tell him what was wrong. Seeing that she had no escape, she then burst into tears and flung herself into Daniel's arms.

She explained that on the night of the craft meeting she had felt low, and accepted the offer of a drink with some of her fellow guild friends, before returning home. Tommy Tobin had been in the pub, drinking heavily, and he had made several comments regarding Tony's inability to service her, and his willingness to do so. Tina became very upset by his taunts. When he repeated the offer, as she went to purchase a round of drinks, she slapped him across the face, as hard as she could. The landlord heard Tommy's remark this time, and immediately threw him out of the pub, barring him at the same time.

Tina then finished her drink and, as the light was now failing, started the ten-minute walk home. As she approached the Tobin farmstead, someone grabbed her from behind and, his arm nearly strangling her, dragged her through a gateway. He then held her down by the throat with one hand, while he raped her.

She did not go to the police, because she did not want Tony to know; she knew that, even in his sick state, he would have killed Tommy. She begged Daniel not to say a word.

Daniel was furious, but gave his word that he would say nothing. Tina already seemed better, simply for having had the chance to tell someone, and even managed a half-smile when they parted.

Daniel was aware that her fears about Tony would have been well-founded, but he himself was not going to let that scumbag get away with this. He had already begun to plan revenge.

With Tommy now banned from the village pub, he had to travel farther away to do his drinking. Daniel monitored his movements, and noted any pattern in his behaviour. For three weeks, every Tuesday, he had taken the bus into Bridport, and not returned until late on the last bus, obviously drunk, by the way that he staggered down the lane.

So, the following Tuesday evening, Daniel waited until near-dark, to drive a pickup down the road and park inside one of Tony's fields. He sat down behind the hedge and waited for nearly two hours, before he heard Tommy scuffling down the road. He waited until Tommy was level with him, before stepping out of the gateway with a hood over his head. Grabbing the man's collar with one hand, Daniel swung him around and delivered a hard right hook to Tommy's jaw. Then, with Tommy out cold, Daniel dragged him behind the hedge and bound his arms and feet, before throwing him in the back of the pick-up.

Daniel drove without lights, swiftly past the entrance to his own home and the dairy, before swinging through a pre-opened gate, along the rough track for over a mile, with little concern for the welfare of the passenger being thrown about behind him. At last, he pulled up beside some old buildings.

Without effort, in one hand he grabbed up the still, limp body from the truck and threw him over his shoulder, before climbing the old, wooden upright ladder, to the hay loft above. Daniel tossed his burden down onto the mat of dusty hay which was the loft's last inhabitant, and waited for Tommy to regain consciousness.

A well-timed emptying of the bladder assisted his cause, and Tommy, disorientated and bound, made several attempts to rise, as his situation became slowly clear to him.

Daniel had donned a mask and gloves, so that even in the dim light of the night sky showing through the sections of clear plastic roofing, Daniel knew that he probably resembled a bank robber or a hangman – from the look of terror in Tommy's eyes, as he became accustomed to the dim light, it was probably the latter.

Daniel prodded him with a boot, making Tommy try to squirm away, before placing the sole heavily on his nether regions. Daniel ensured that Tommy was well aware of why he was there, and disguising his voice with a thick Irish accent, took great delight in explaining what he was going to do to Tommy. When he got to the bit about the boy's testicles falling off after a week, Tommy passed out.

Daniel was enjoying the scenario. He would have much rather

have killed the little rat, but that would have been too quick, and he wanted to make him suffer. He threw a cup of water into Tommy's face, rousing him, then dragged him to the centre of the floor, where lay a prepared rack. He unfastened the temporary rope bonds and replaced them with the padded chain fetters fastened to the rack, placing a gag in Tommy's mouth.

Daniel then undid the belt on Tommy's trousers, commenting on the fact that he had wet himself, as he pulled his trousers down to his ankles. He made sure that Tommy was watching as he placed the rubber ring on the castrating tool. Tommy squirmed, wriggled and screamed as loud as the gag would allow him, but Daniel just calmly reached out, pulled one testicle down in the scrotum and let the tool close, depositing its ring firmly in place. Tommy passed out again, as he finished the second.

But Daniel waited for him to stir; he wasn't finished yet. When he did, Daniel caught a small piece of his foreskin and placed another ring on that, explaining to Tommy that he had put it on his penis; he was now going to stick a pipe down Tommy's throat and keep pouring water into him until his bladder burst, because he would not be able to urinate. From the sudden smell, though, he could at least still use his bowels, and Daniel had to move away until the air cleared a little. Daniel made a half-hearted attempt to carry out his threat, even though he knew it wouldn't work if he couldn't put the third ring on properly – but in truth the stench was too strong, and his efforts would have little effect other than to create more fear.

So, instead, Daniel removed the gag from Tommy's mouth,

making clear that he was so far from any habitation that no one would hear him scream, so to do so would be a waste of his energy. He then placed a container of water with a straw sticking out of it within reach, and promised to be back in the morning to feed him – if the rats didn't get him first. Daniel could hear Tommy's muttered pleas, as he climbed down the stairs and got into the truck.

The first thing he did was remove the mask and wipe the sweat from his face, before driving slowly back along the rutted track, only putting on his lights when he passed the buildings.

Daniel kept Tommy there for three days, until he could stand the stench of him no longer. Then, as dark fell, he replaced the chains with rope and placed a bag over his captive's head, before lowering him through the loft hatch to the floor below.

Once down himself, he right-hooked Tommy under the jaw again, before removing the bag and tossing the unconscious lad without ceremony into the back of the truck. Daniel drove him back to the same place from where he had abducted him. With the mask back on, he removed the bonds, threatening Tommy with death if he told anyone what had happened to him, before sinking a solid blow into his solar plexus, felling him once again.

Daniel drove on toward the village, knowing that he would be out of sight before his victim had enough wind back in his body to stand up and see the vehicle he had been transported in, let alone read its registration.

Daniel did not see Tommy for over a week after that, and when he did he was walking very stiffly. Nobody mentioned a word about his ordeal, so it was obvious that he hadn't told anyone.

Daniel knew that he would have lost any feeling in his testicles shortly after he had put the rings on but, unlike a lamb, wasn't sure how long they would take to fall off. But, fall off they did – or, at least, the first one did, unfortunately before it was really ready to, and with the help of a knee from some lad he was annoying in a Bridport bar. An ambulance was called when blood seeped through his jeans, as he lay prone on the floor, and it was in hospital that the truth had been discovered. The second was removed in a more sterile manner.

The police had been notified and Tommy questioned, but very little was learnt from their interview. Firstly, Tommy would have had to incriminate himself and admit to rape and, secondly, although he probably had an idea, he had no proof of his assailant's identity.

A local cop, who lived in the village, let it slip after several pints whilst off duty, and the news spread like wildfire. Speculation on why someone had done this to him, or even if he had done it to himself, ran wild, but as no one knew the real reason for his plight, no one came near to guessing it.

But, Daniel was very aware that once Tina heard the gossip, she would know of a bloody good reason, and would be after him for answers. He managed to avoid her for nearly a week, and even then slipped away from a visit to Tony whilst she was on the phone, leaving her no chance to catch him on his own. He knew she had heard about Tommy's situation just by looking into her eyes. While she made supper, Tina indicated with a movement of her head for Daniel to follow her into the kitchen. He pretended not to see and avoided looking at her directly, even though from the corner of his eye he could see her trying to attract his attention, until he managed to escape.

Daniel should have known it wouldn't be that easy, with a woman of Tina's determination, and it was of little surprise that he found her sat at his own kitchen table the following breakfast time, with Alice nowhere to be seen. Daniel could remember the conversation which followed, vividly.

Tina offered to make his toast, and took his already prepared breakfast from the AGA warming oven, placing it on the table while he washed his hands. As she poured his coffee, she then said two words: "Tommy Tobin."

The conversation then progressed something like this:

"What about him?"

"Someone castrated him."

"Did they?"

"What do you know about it?"

"Why should I know anything about it?"

"Instead of all these questions, look me in the eye and tell me you know nothing about it."

Daniel once again refused to meet her eyes.

"Look at me! Look at me!!" Tina's voice had now risen several octaves higher.

Daniel lifted his head and looked directly into her eyes; he didn't answer, but he knew the truth was in his own.

"You did this for me?" Her voice was now soft, her eyes moistening.

"For you and Tony," Daniel answered, quietly. "He mustn't know. Nor Alice; she mustn't know, either."

"She won't, unless you tell her. Thank you." She walked around the table, kissed him softly atop his head and left.

A problem now lay in the fact that the whole village knew about Tommy. Although Tony eventually got to hear about it, the information meant little above face value to him, and he barely mentioned it in conversation. The real problem lay in the fact that no one liked Tommy, his father or his brothers. The male population of the village tended to start whistling "Colonel Bogey's Theme", with the youngers making up their own words, while the females blatantly teased him for sex, or made some other ridiculing remark.

It was after a few weeks of this that Jimmy Tobin was released from prison – and he soon became aware of what had happened to his son.

It was later learnt that he had virtually beaten a name out of Tommy – it was, of course, Daniel's name which was put forward as prime suspect. Jimmy didn't care to hear the reason that Tommy suspected Daniel, simply rushing out to look for him, instead.

Daniel had been to rugby practice, and was supping his second pint in the local pub afterward, when Jimmy burst in wielding a tyre lever. Daniel disarmed him with ease, then broke his arm with the weapon, before sending him flying across several tables, with a well-placed straight right to the chin, which rendered him unconscious.

There were several other customers in the bar, as well as his own teammates, and they had all heard Jimmy's ranting as he entered the pub, followed by more when he had come around. Even after he had been escorted outside and banned, he continued to rant and rave outside an open window. In the end, the barmaid called the police – and Daniel's problems really started.

Naturally, Daniel's fellow drinkers were keen for an explanation, as well as the police. Daniel dismissed it all, denying any knowledge of what Jimmy was talking about. When the police questioned other patrons, none suggested that Daniel had done anything more than disarm Jimmy and punch him once. Either they hadn't seen Daniel give Jimmy's arm a heavy blow with the tyre lever, or had deliberately failed to mention it.

Having given the police a statement, Daniel returned home, calling in briefly to warn Tina of the latest developments. Luckily, Tony was dozing and didn't even know that he had been there. Unfortunately, it was not to stay that way for much longer.

Jimmy's incessant ranting to the police ensured that they once again looked into it, and under questioning Tommy admitted that he had raped Tina. He told them his side of the story as he knew it, including his suspicion that it was Daniel who had kidnapped and castrated him.

The police waited until the following morning. The local

bobbies, knowing about Tony's illness, called Tina and asked her if she would prefer to go to the police station to help with their enquiries, regarding a reported incident.

Tina immediately rushed to see Daniel in a panic; being aware of the previous evening's events, she knew full well what they were enquiring about. Daniel offered to go with her, but she refused, saying that would make his guilt appear more obvious. So, armed with Daniel's assurance that they had no proof, she set off for Bridport.

Once the police had ascertained that she had been raped, they asked her if Daniel was aware of the rape, and if she thought he would have inflicted this punishment on Tommy. She admitted that she had confided the rape to him, and they had agreed that no one else should know, with Tony being so ill.

Before she could even get back to warn Daniel, the police had pulled him in for questioning. Daniel immediately stated that he was unaware of the rape, directly contradicting Tina's statement, though he agreed that Tina would not have wanted Tony to know – not only because of his cancer, but also the fact that he would probably have taken the law into his own hands, and ended his days in prison.

Daniel knew the interviewing officers and, immediately once the tape had been turned off, they warned him that Tina had already told them what he had known. Still, for the time being, he had not been accused of anything, and Daniel was free to go.

Meanwhile, Tommy was charged with rape and Jimmy with assault; both would appear before the local magistrates the following day.

Because Jimmy was already on parole, he was consequently recalled to prison, with an additional three months added. However, for some peculiar reason, Tommy was allowed bail until his case went to court. When Tommy's solicitor asked for a copy of Tina's statement, both copies of the tape had mysteriously disappeared.

By now, Tony knew the whole truth from Tina, and continually thanked Daniel every time he saw him. He swore to never tell anyone.

Tommy was now the subject of even more ridicule and, once the story had spread to Bridport and beyond, he had nowhere to hide. Rancorous laughter followed him everywhere he dared show his face, and if he wasn't being threatened with violence, he had to outrun cutting abuse. Remarks about his sexuality and how he would be treated in prison seemed to affect him the most, and triggered him screaming insults back at his persecutors.

His trial was fixed for mid-December, and he remained out on bail, his barrister having convinced the judge that he was no longer a threat and was needed at home.

Two days before the start of the trial, he went to Dorchester with his brother for a few drinks. Unfortunately, there were some lads from the village out there, for a change of scenery, and Tommy had the misfortune of running into them almost immediately. The lads took great delight in pointing Tommy out to everyone they could. Fearing for his life, he had returned home.

Once his brothers were in bed that night, he wrote a note and crept out to the barn. His younger brother found him the following morning, hanging from a beam; the ladder he had used to climb up there lay on the floor beneath him. Suicide was obvious.

A week later he was cremated, with only his brothers, father and accompanying prison officers present. The local press made a brief mention in the weekly rag, and both Daniel and Tina then thought that would be the end of things.

What was not immediately evident was that either Jimmy or one of the Tobins' briefs could smell something fishy, and put pressure on the force who had been drafted in to investigate the disappearing tapes from Tina's interview, which had initially ended without any answers, due to a lack of evidence.

The Devon and Cornwall force was called in to try and find the truth, and this time they seemed determined to do so. Tina underwent several interviews and, although the officers made it quite clear that they did not suspect her of harming Tommy, they also made it evident that they knew it was connected, and were confident that she knew the assailant. Daniel's name had more than once cropped up in the interviews, and even though the tapes of her original interview had been "lost" before they could be transcribed, they dwelt heavily on the fact that she had told the officers Daniel had been made aware of the rape, when he had originally denied it. At that point, her brief had instructed her to say nothing, but she was well aware of their thinking, by the questions they asked.

She warned Daniel, who was surprised that they hadn't already pulled him in for requestioning first. The first Daniel knew of their interest being renewed was the arrival of at least a dozen police vehicles, with a search warrant for all the farm buildings on the estate. It transpired later that, from Tommy's statement, it was clear that the distance from where he had been held captive to the field in which he was released was fairly short, because he could remember looking at his watch before being knocked out, then looking at it again when he came around in the field; the time difference showed that his castration had occurred not far away. With Daniel the main suspect, and his land being adjacent, his buildings were an obvious place to start.

Daniel had dismantled the rack he had built to hold Tommy, and this had been burnt, along with the blankets he had covered his victim with. He had forgotten to dispose of the plastic pipe he used to intimidate Tommy further, and it lay in a corner of the barn, where he had thrown it. This, along with other bits and pieces, was taken, and found to contain both Daniel's and Tommy's D.N.A.

Daniel was again pulled in for questioning, and this time later charged with kidnapping, false imprisonment and causing grievous bodily harm. He was told that further charges could be forthcoming.

Neither Daniel nor his solicitor David Beam were too concerned at this stage, as any evidence they had was only circumstantial. Even so, Daniel had been brought up to "tell the truth and shame the Devil," and was not very happy about lying – not that he had said very much in the interview, once he could see where their line of questioning was leading. It was not until he answered bail two weeks later, and was charged with involuntary manslaughter, that both Daniel and his brief took the charges seriously.

David immediately engaged a barrister from London, with a glowing reputation, and once the trial date had been set for late July, the three of them met to discuss the case. Daniel was pre-warned that the barrister could only present to the court what Daniel was minded to tell him, and it would be ethically impossible to defend him if he was aware of any facts which contradicted his plea. Daniel stuck to his innocent plea and told them nothing.

By this time, Tony was failing fast, almost skeletal and drugged heavily, to alleviate the pain which now wracked his entire body. It had been decided to keep the trial from him, and it was just eighteen days before it commenced that Tony finally succumbed.

During the final week, Daniel sat with him when Tina tried to sleep. Knowing the end was near, he stayed with Tina that day. It was about six in the evening that Tony drew his last visible breath.

Both Tony's and her own parents were present, but luckily the children had been with Tina's sister for a week. Even with them there, she had not wanted him to leave before the end. Tina had eventually told them of her ordeal, but had not disclosed Daniel's part in it.

Daniel, realizing that if found guilty he needed to have his affairs in order, had invited Richard and Jen over for supper a few weeks previously, and with Alice also present, had told them the full story. Although they were aware of some of the facts, and had indeed wondered if he might have been the culprit, still they were shocked by his frank confession. Each swore to keep it to themselves, and

Daniel never doubted that they would do otherwise. He was glad to get it off his chest.

Four days after Tony's death, he was buried in the village churchyard. Daniel was one of the pallbearers, along with three of his fellow football buddies. The church was jam-packed, and hundreds more listened to the service relayed on loudspeakers outside. The wake was held at the village pub, and luckily the weather was fine, as it was too small inside to accommodate the throng which had come to repay their respects.

Tina's father supported her during the service but, after two hours at the wake, she asked Daniel to take her home. She declined her parents' offer to go with them, stating that she wanted to be alone. But, when they arrived at her home, she begged Daniel to keep her company for a while. Daniel obliged.

Whilst Tina was showering and changing out of the suit she had worn to the funeral, into something more to her liking, he made them both a strong coffee. Then, Tina talked and Daniel listened.

Tina asked for a glass of wine, then another, insisting that Daniel join her. This appeared to make her weepy. Daniel suggested that she come home with him, and let Alice take care of her, but again she was insistent that she wanted to be in her own home that night.

Daniel had by now removed his suit waistcoat and jacket, as well as the black tie; his top buttons were now undone and his shirt sleeves rolled above his elbows, making him feel a lot more relaxed. He was in the kitchen, in the midst of uncorking their third bottle, when Tina came to him, asking for a cuddle. Daniel held her close, her head buried in his chest.

Suddenly she reached up, entwined her arms around his neck and kissed him passionately. Whose fault it was that things went farther was not clear, but she began ripping his clothes off, as he lifted her jumper over her head and released the button on her skirt, letting it fall to the floor. Her hands were immediately inside his Y-fronts as he released the hooks on her bra, and she already had his pants down to his knees and his cock in her hand, as he lifted her onto the kitchen table, his mouth seeking out a hardened nipple. She pulled the flimsy G-string to one side and guided him into her.

Daniel lifted her up, the two of them still coupled, and lay her upon the settee as, without stopping, he continued to pound into her. Her legs were now wrapped tightly around his waist and, with a scream which would have brought anyone within earshot running, she bucked wildly as she climaxed, bringing Daniel to his a split-second later.

Still not satisfied, she then took Daniel by the hand and led him to her bed. It was only after the third copulation that she fell asleep.

Daniel was used to drinking and, by now, even with the copious amount he had consumed, the effects had worn off; the guilt now kicked in. Slipping his arm from beneath the now snoring Tina, he rose, dressed quietly and left.

Even in his own bed he could not sleep. When he did drop off, he woke with the evening's events still firmly on his mind, the guilt almost intolerable. Some of the last words Tony said to him were to promise to look after Tina and the kids – well, he'd made a bloody good start!

Daniel asked Alice to phone Tina in the morning and check on her wellbeing. But, after a short conversation, Alice summoned Daniel through to the hall to take the phone.

Tina took the blame for the previous evening's events and told him not to feel guilty; what they had done could not be undone, and Tony would have understood. Still, Tina might have been able to put it aside, but Daniel could not.

He took Alice with him the following day, to check up on Tina and the children, who were now home. When he arrived, he saw that one of the local C.I.D. officers was just leaving. Daniel had seen him there several times, even when Tony was alive, so when Tina told them he had just called in to check she was okay, Daniel dismissed it as irrelevant.

The happenings of the day of the funeral were not mentioned by either of them, although there was an obvious awkwardness, and both made sure they didn't get too close this time.

On the day of the trial, Daniel and his team were fairly confident that, whatever the Crown came up with, there was no real evidence that Daniel was implicated in any way, and that the jury would find him not guilty – if the case was not discharged before it had even gone that far.

Still, right from the very start, the judge seemed to have it in for Daniel. Whenever he could, he twisted things: the fact that Daniel played rugby made him a thug; the fact he had been born into a wealthy family made him a silver-spooned yob; objections sustained or overruled were always apparently one-sided. With the name Jeffreys, Daniel couldn't help but wonder if he was a direct descendant of the infamous Judge Jeffreys, who had presided over a reign of terror in the same Dorchester court, over three centuries earlier. Still, relative or not, Daniel knew that he was in for a hard time.

Calls for dismissal were quickly shunned, but to all intents and purposes, the case appeared to be going nowhere – until the Crown called Tina to give evidence. Daniel's team protested, on the grounds that she was in an unfit state to do so, following the recent loss of her husband, but the judge once again denied the defence's request, as if hoping that something would emerge to discredit Daniel. Daniel was watching the judge when the Crown prosecutor hit the jackpot, and actually saw the smile appear on his face, his lips nearly curling up to his ears.

The prosecutor was giving Tina a hard time, and continually pressed her on Daniel's possible involvement, when she cracked and shouted back at the prosecutor that Daniel had only done it so that Tony didn't find out about the rape. Asked to repeat herself, she realized her mistake, and tried to twist what she had said into a scenario: only that *if* he had done it, it would be so Tony wouldn't find out.

But it was too late: she had said it and the whole court had heard her. The judge immediately called for a recess, and called both legal teams to his chambers.

The prognosis was bad; Daniel was advised to plead guilty on the original charges, but let events after the fact go to the jury. Daniel accepted their advice, even though the sentence for these could theoretically be as bad as that for murder. But, considering the extraordinary circumstances, they were sure that the judge would go easy on him. Daniel himself wasn't so sure.

After changing his plea, the jury found him not guilty on the manslaughter charge.

With some difficulty, and again with some resistance from the judge rather than the prosecutor, Daniel was reluctantly given the time to get his affairs in order before sentencing.

That day was now here.

Daniel looked down at his watch. It was time to go.

He arose, lit the last of the cigars, whistled up the dogs. Then, with a last glance around him, he set off down the hill.

7

DANIEL COULD SMELL the breakfast cooking as he approached the kitchen door. He didn't feel at all hungry, but he knew that Alice would think he needed a good one – and, as things stood, it would probably be the last decent breakfast he would get for a while.

Daniel washed the dogs' feet off, with the hose by the back door, and wiped their feet before letting them in. The kitchen had a flagged floor, and to all of them apart from Jessie, the rest of the house was off-limits without invitation. The kitchen was huge, so the space their baskets took up, on one side of the AGA, wasn't missed.

Daniel could see that Alice had been crying again, and swiftly made his escape to shower and change. He also scooped off the soiled bedding and placed it in the wash-basket, along with his dirty clothes. Daniel placed his best watch in the safe and replaced it with a cheap one, but decided to keep his father's signet ring on, before picking up the case, already packed in preparation for his incarceration. He also returned and transferred his money into an old, tatty wallet, which he could never quite work out why he had retained. Then, he picked up the case again and set off down the stairs. He left the case in the hallway, rather than place it where Alice could see it.

He didn't feel hungry, but he ate the extra-large fry-up she had prepared. She fussed over him like a broody hen, hardly waiting for his coffee cup to empty before rushing to refill, or the last portion on his plate to disappear into his mouth, before the plate was removed and a plateful of toast placed before him.

The phone rang as he was eating his second slice and Alice answered it, returning a few minutes later to tell him that Tina had just rung to wish him luck, but was not going to the court to hear sentencing. Tina felt it was her fault that Daniel now faced prison, even though he had tried to explain that the actions had been his alone; all she had done was tell the truth.

Daniel had called in to see her two evenings earlier, to give the kids a present, and found the same C.I.D. officer sitting in the front room with them; he had still been there when Daniel left. Tina phoned a short time later, explaining that he was an old teammate of Tony's, who had stopped playing after a knee injury, and had at one time been a frequent visitor. Perhaps he was only an old friend, but Daniel wasn't too sure.

Daniel asked Alice for one of the Senior Service Plain she still smoked, and went outside the back door to smoke it. Alice followed him and wrapped her arm around his waist, while Daniel put his arm around her shoulder and pulled her to him. Alice then started to cry, and Daniel did his best to console her. When their cigarettes were finished, she pulled him into a full embrace. Daniel loved this woman like a mother, and treated her as such; he hated what he was putting her through.

A horn sounded out the front. With one last cuddle he broke from her embrace, retrieved his case and, without looking back, made his way out of the house, to where Richard stood beside the waiting car.

Driving through the village, signs had been posted on every available post or gate, wishing him well; those at home waved and women blew him kisses. Even on the main road to Dorchester, signs had been placed bearing similar slogans.

Arriving at the court, some forty minutes later, a throng had gathered outside, along with the paparazzi. Cheers and well wishes were shouted, as cameras flashed. Daniel ignored requests for interviews and made his way inside, where he found David Beam waiting to usher him to a meeting with his barrister.

Although all of the things Daniel had been convicted of carried a maximum life sentence, it was not expected that he would receive more than six years, the circumstances being what they were. With remission and time off for good behaviour, Daniel would be hard done by if he served more than three years at most.

A cup of coffee and a scrounged cigarette later, it was time to hand himself in and experience his first taste of a cell. Luckily, they had no objection to David staying with him, until it was almost time for him to be led, handcuffed, to his place in the dock.

Daniel's belly had felt queasy all morning, but the glare he received from Judge Jeffreys, as he entered the courtroom, sent shivers down his spine and made his whole body shudder.

His barrister read out a prewritten statement, in which Daniel refused to apologize for what he had done and, even now, facing a lengthy sentence, declared that he would still do it again. Of course, the barrister was loath to say that, but Daniel had made him promise not to deliberately go against his wishes.

Now, though, Daniel's heart sank lower with every word the judge uttered, and in his head he added a year to his sentence for every cutting remark. The people in the public gallery had gone totally silent, as if stunned by some of the remarks the judge was coming out with.

However, they were more shocked by the sentence he handed down. He proclaimed that he had taken into consideration the guilty plea, yet sentenced Daniel to fifteen years for kidnapping, ten for false imprisonment and fifteen for causing grievous bodily harm.

He added a final remark that, regardless of what the jury had found him not guilty of, Tommy Tobin would still be alive today, albeit in prison, if Daniel had not taken the law into his own hands. Then, with the spectators still in an uproar, Jeffreys banged his gavel for order, and shouted for Daniel to be taken down. Even the court officials and two officers who led him away looked totally flabbergasted.

As Daniel slumped down on the bed in the holding cell, his legal team came rushing in, blubbering about applying for an appeal immediately. But Daniel was too shocked to really take in what they were saying.

8

DANIEL WAS KEPT in the cell until the end of court proceedings for the day, before being handcuffed again and taken to a waiting prison van. From the noise as they set off, it was obvious that a large crowd had remained outside the court to vent their opinions on British justice, and calls of encouragement could be heard as the van slowly made its way through the throng.

The sentence handed down was now starting to really sink in; Daniel considered he would be lucky to be out before he turned forty.

A fellow prisoner told him that they were on their way to Shaftesbury's Guys Marsh Prison. This fellow had been there before, and told Daniel that it wasn't a bad place, though this did little to raise Daniel's spirits. The journey passed almost in silence.

Daniel simply followed orders as he passed through the reception area, and hardly noticed that the handcuffs had now been removed. He barely listened to the briefing he and his fellow traveller received, before he was soon whisked away. Daniel fell in behind the prison officer designated to take him to his cell.

As they passed the recreation area, a loud cheer went up.

The screw turned around and said: "You'll be fine here; they think you're a bloody hero."

This was of little interest to Daniel. What would have been, had he been aware of it, was the fact that Jimmy Tobin had been released from this very same prison that morning, and was now sat at his kitchen table with his surviving son, plotting revenge.

Daniel was given a single cell, and told he would only be there for a few days, until they had evaluated him – what he found out later meant to assess if he was a suicide risk; Daniel was relieved to be alone. Once he had made his bed, he lay down and tried to shut out the noise of banging doors and voices, which seemed to echo from cells farther down the line, as inmates tried to hold conversations with their neighbours. Some of the shouting was directed at him, but he was in no mood to engage in small talk and ignored it. The only thing which brought a shred of cheer to him was the fact that there was a window, through the bars of which he could see the sky.

He was wondering if he could survive what would probably be the next twelve years in a place like this, when he was brought back to reality by the clanging of a hatch in his cell door, and a voice informing him that his food was there. Daniel retrieved the tray and tried to eat the bland food he now had resting on his lap. His hunger wasn't great, and this certainly wasn't appetising enough to tempt him; the tea was nearly cold and like dishwater. Daniel put the tray to one side.

As he lay on his bed, he could hear a radio playing one of his favourite songs, in a vehicle in the car park, and strained his ears to listen. Daniel loved music, and sighed in acceptance that it would be a long time before he would drive, singing along to a song, as the air whistled past, his arm resting on the open window. He had soared like an eagle; now he felt like a budgerigar – less even than a canary.

Daniel stayed in his cell for three days, with only brief excursions outside for food and exercise.

Richard took up the option of the induction visit, but did nothing to raise Daniel's spirits, as he spent more time bewailing his friend's fate and conditions than anything else.

On the fourth day, Daniel was instructed to pack his things and was moved to a normal wing, where once again he was relieved to find that he had been allocated a cell on his own – a double, in fact. It soon became fairly obvious that it was not only the inmates, but also the staff who considered him harshly treated; they had not only put him on enhanced status almost immediately, but went beyond. Warders would come and chat with him, and would leave behind a nearly full pack of cigarettes or sweets when they left. Anything that he mentioned he liked would appear in the cell whilst he was out.

He was given a job outside, in the gardens. Daniel was glad to be able to escape the smells and noises of the inside, and felt sorry for those restricted to it, day and night.

David paid him regular legal visits and, as Richard had power of attorney, the wing governor suggested that they could come in together, so his visiting orders might be saved for others. They even allowed non-legal papers through, so Daniel was able to get a lot of farm-related paperwork in, without going through the normal channels. Tina requested that she be sent a visiting order, but with so much time on his hands, Daniel had started to blame her for his predicament, and sent back a message saying that he didn't want to see her.

He spoke to Alice regularly, and understood the fact that she couldn't face coming to see him. But she sent in little food parcels with Richard, which again he was able to keep without any restriction.

Alone at night, Daniel couldn't sleep. He was used to being physically and mentally tired, but now he had little to tax his body or mind. Dwelling on his present situation, he began to resent Tina more and more; if it hadn't been for her, he wouldn't be here. He also dwelt on the night of the funeral and felt sick about it. It had been Tina who threw herself at him. In some ways he could understand if it had only been the once, but she had led him to her bed – or, rather, Tony's bed – before he became really ill, and wanted more. Daniel hated himself for what he had done – even more so that it gave him an erection to remember her soft, willing body.

But she had let her tongue slip in court, and the more he thought about it, the more he hated and despised her.

9

ABOUT SIX WEEKS into his sentence, Daniel had come to something like acceptance of his fate and, lying in his bed, his thoughts returned to the fairer sex. This was definitely the longest he had been without a woman, and one evening, for the first time since his arrival, he felt himself getting aroused.

His hand slipped beneath the covers and into his boxer shorts, his member stiffening until it was straining for release. Eventually, unable to contain himself any longer, he committed to satisfying himself. It definitely gave him some relief, even though his blanket now had a large, wet patch, and a musky odour filled the air.

The situation reminded him of a scenario many years earlier, and Daniel's mind went back to the first time he had done that – or rather, something like it. He was about twelve and a half. It was a Sunday, and in Daniel's house the Sabbath was strictly observed; no more was to be done than necessary, and even the children were told to spend the day quietly, writing or reading – preferably the Bible – but definitely no games. Daniel had gone to the bathroom, accompanied as usual by his shadow, Elsie. Daniel rolled a sheet of toilet paper into a ball and tossed it to her, at which she lay on the bathmat and contentedly began to desiccate the tissue.

Once he had finished his business, Daniel flushed the toilet, but stayed seated and began to examine his penis. As he twisted and turned it, it started to become aroused, and the more Daniel played with it, the bigger it became. Daniel started to stroke the underside, which now appeared to have a raised vein standing proud. It was now about eight inches in length, and standing stiffly, with a slight throbbing movement. Daniel could see with the helmet partially covered in some white matter, and as he rubbed it, this started to come away. Daniel smelt it; it was definitely rank and cheesy.

His stroking and probing the sensitive area took him to a plateau he had never experienced before. His body started to jerk spasmodically and uncontrollably, and a stream of thick, white stuff ejaculated in spurts, each jerk almost hitting the wall on the other side of the bathroom, as his back banged against the toilet seat in unison with each spasm. Seeing the spurts, Elsie jumped up trying to catch it as it shot overhead, catching some, with the following salvo landing on her long coat.

The feeling had been unbelievable, and the air filled with a strong and musty odour he would never forget. As his penis slowly slackened off, Daniel continued to pull back his foreskin, cleaning the cheesy mess off as it stretched. In so doing, he had made it bleed slightly, where the foreskin joined at the back.

Daniel learnt three things that night: he understood what was required for circumcision, about which he had read so often in the Bible, and the reason for it; he now knew what Alice had meant when, as a child, she would ask him if he had washed it properly; and also that playing with himself gave him great satisfaction.

Later that evening, after chapel, Daniel repeated his previous experience with a little more gusto and a definite hand action. Again he had bled a little, so, even though he aroused himself in the morning, he left it until he was in the bath that night, before he did it again. This time he found that the sperm had settled on his legs, leaving flaky stuff to wipe off as he dried.

From that day, he had masturbated two or three times a day until he started having sex with girls, when he eventually found no need to satisfy himself. That was, until tonight.

Daniel joined any course he could, if it kept him from the cell, including one on farm and estate management – where it soon became clear to his tutor that Daniel was the one who should be doing the teaching. He got on well with his fellow inmates and joined in all the recreational periods, but how he missed his freedom, and hated the rigid regime they had to adhere to.

Christmas was now on the horizon, which saddened him more. Daniel loved giving, as well as the parties with his friends; all that beckoned here, by all accounts, was more time locked up.

Still, he had plenty to keep him occupied, as the Parsons now wanted to retire completely. Daniel had moved the milking cows three years before, to lighten their load, and replaced them with a suckler herd and a flock of sheep. The neighbouring farm had been sold for housing development, and open gates, cut fences and dumped rubbish were just some of the problems they now faced.

The last straw had been when the stock bull had broken out and run amok. Luckily, no one had been hurt, but several cars had felt the force of his head. A police marksman had eventually shot the bull, to prevent anyone being gored. The knackerman who was present at the time then made a startling discovery: someone had been using the bull's testicles for target practice; in fact, he later recovered fifteen air-rifle pellets from them, and several more from its flanks. The police did find the culprit: a fifteen-year-old lad who had received the air rifle as a birthday present; his parents were fined and the lad sent to a youth offenders' institution for a few months.

Howard Austin negotiated a really good price for the majority of the farm to be developed, and they had agreed to Daniel's demands that the old farmhouse was not included, nor the orchard and two small paddocks behind it. This block would be totally enclosed by an eight-foot brick and rail wall, so the Parsons could spend their retirement there.

Howard told him that Bluebell Wood was also causing similar problems, since the adjoining farm had been sold for building and the local council were considering compulsory purchase, after their efforts to purchase had been turned down on several occasions. Daniel had an idea which would preserve the area – one that he felt his father would have been in agreement with, in view of this threat – and at the same time utilize the ground efficiently. Ordnance Survey maps were brought in and Daniel spent his free time working on his ideas, while Richard was instructed to look for more farms or estates, even outside Dorset, if suitable. He booked a visit two days before

Christmas, along with two of his old teammates, and Daniel was hoping to have a rough draft done for him by then.

Having achieved this, he waited with anticipation for them to arrive, and was surprised to see Richard come in on his own. From the expression on Richard's face, Daniel could sense that something was wrong. Richard blurted out that Tina's house had been burnt down the previous night, and that it was Jimmy Tobin and his lad who had done it. After ascertaining that Tina and her children were safe, Daniel calmed Richard down and got a fuller story.

Apparently, at about two a.m., Tina had woken to a loud bang and the smell of smoke. Thinking back later, she said that it was probably the noise of something being thrown through the window which had awoken her. Opening the bedroom door, she could see the reflection of flames coming from the hall area.

She ventured partway down, and could see that there was little chance of getting down that way safely. So, she woke the children and made for the back stairs. The smell of smoke was strong there also, and on reaching the kitchen she could see that the back door was also ablaze, but had not yet spread into the room. She went to open the lounge door, intending to exit through the French windows, but that too was well alight. Luckily, there was a door leading directly into the garage from the laundry room, and it was through this that she escaped.

She then realized that she had forgotten her mobile phone, left beside the bed and, with the children safely in the car, she ventured back into the house to use the landline in the passage from the kitchen, but found the line dead. She drove as fast as she safely could to Daniel's house and woke Alice.

Unfortunately, by the time the fire brigade reached it, the house was totally gutted. The police found the Tobins' van stuck in a ditch, just outside the entrance to the farm; from the tyre marks, it appeared that someone had reversed out of the drive and misjudged the width of the verge, toppling straight into the ditch. From the mud spatter, it was clear that the driver had made frantic efforts to free the van, without success. Opening the rear doors revealed several empty cans, which had certainly contained petrol. The police knew straight away that the van was the Tobins', and arrested them immediately.

Tina and the children were staying with Alice for the time being, so she could still run the farm, but she was in a very distressed state, having lost all of their personal belongings, including those which she had kept throughout her life with Tony. Daniel sympathized with her; he still treasured many things himself regarding his lost family – anything perishable he kept in a fireproof box in his safe.

Daniel's two friends then made their appearance and tried to liven up the mood, but the conversation always returned to the Tobins, for one reason or another.

When visiting was over, Daniel had to wait to call Alice, who was herself in a distressed state, even though no one had been hurt. Daniel was just grateful that had been the case; he could remember well how she had reacted following the plane crash.

Daniel agreed that it was fine to let Tina, Sam, Timmy and Victoria stay there, until they could get themselves sorted. Tony had the older two children christened also, when he knew his fate, and Daniel had been asked to be godfather to them, as well. Daniel loved them, and was pleased to be able to give Tony some comfort, knowing that he took the privilege and responsibility of being a godparent seriously. Even so, he still felt bitter toward Tina, and didn't wish to speak to her – though he did pass on his commiserations, through Alice.

When Daniel spoke to Alice on Christmas Day, she had returned to her normal self, fretting about him in the main. He also spoke to the children, who were ecstatic about the presents Richard and Alice had bought them on his behalf – all that their mother had wrapped for them were destroyed in the fire.

Between Christmas and the New Year several things occurred, in what, according to the longer serving inmates, was usually a quiet time.

Tom Jenkins, the wing governor, came to Daniel and asked him if he was racist in any way. Once Daniel had assured him he was not, Tom went on to explain that space was now tight, and that they would probably have to give him a cellmate. In the induction wing was a young, mixed-race fellow who, according to Tom, wasn't really a bad kid, but had a cocky, mouthy attitude, which would not serve him well in prison. Daniel was asked if he would not only have him as a cellmate, but also try and keep him from getting hurt.

Tom returned later with a second request. Ken "Diddy" Hodges, who took the estate management course, had been severely injured in a car accident, having been hit by a drunken driver, and definitely would not be back at work for several months. Would Daniel take over the instruction? Daniel agreed.

Within two minutes, Daniel could see why Tom had been concerned about his new cellmate: Bobby Brown swaggered into the cell as if he owned the place, rather than being there at Her Majesty's pleasure. He immediately demanded the top bunk.

Tom winked at Daniel, nodded to the other officer present to leave and, with a shake of his head, followed him out of the cell.

Daniel had already forgotten the kid's name and took to calling him "Chalky", while explaining that the top bunk was his, and there was no way he was sleeping on the bottom bunk, with someone farting above him. Gas, he explained, drifted along the ground, so whoever slept on the bottom would receive the biggest dose.

Chalky acted like a cock bantam at this: voice high pitched and arms flailing around. Daniel invited him to take a swing, and when he tried, Daniel easily parried the haymaker, sinking his own hard into Chalky's solar plexus.

When Chalky had recovered his breath and stopped calling Daniel names – some of which he had never heard before – Daniel suggested that they try again. Introducing himself, he offered Chalky his hand. Chalky eventually accepted it, though still muttering under his breath.

In the first recreation period after this, Daniel twice had to intervene as Chalky rubbed fellow inmates up the wrong way; he was glad when it was finally over. He didn't even make his usual phone call to Richard or Alice, so sure was he that trouble would start as soon as he had turned his back. He had to admit that Chalky had a sense of humour, but it appeared to be at others' expense. His banter might have been accepted amongst friends, but in this place... definitely not! He would have to teach Chalky a few manners before someone else did.

That evening, alone in the cell, Chalky opened up. As he had no cigarettes, a few roll-ups were enough to get his engagement. For Chalky, this was his first time in prison, but he had been in trouble for most of his life. He hadn't known his father, but had always seemed to have lots of uncles. His mother had taken to drink and drugs, though Chalky swore to Daniel that, to this day, he had never been drunk or even taken any drugs – not even a joint – though he did admit to dealing them. In his opinion, the only dealers who made any money were the ones who didn't use. His sister had been born when he was six years old and, once again, no one could be sure who the father was, other than she was mixed-race, like himself.

As Chalky grew a little older, he learned that his mother was using her body to get the things she wanted. Often there was no food in the house, so he started stealing from the local shops to feed himself and his little sister. His mother would often disappear for several days at a time, leaving him to fend for himself and Sofia. Then she would return, hardly knowing where she was or what day it was. Things improved a little for a few years, after his mother won £25,000 playing bingo. She rented a little house near Acton and smartened herself up. Eventually the money ran out, but by then she had smartened herself up enough that she was able to get a job with an escort agency. Initially this went well, but as she took more drugs and drank more, she lost regular customers because of her appearance, and also a tendency to cause trouble whilst in a drunken state; things quickly reverted to a life as before.

Chalky started to sell some gear for one of his mother's dealers, as well as stealing anything he could sell for a few pounds. He committed burglary, pickpocketing, auto theft and shoplifting, but stressed that he had never used violence or taken from those who could not afford to lose it. He said he hadn't been very good at it, as he was always getting caught.

His mother sunk to a new low, when she started using heavier class-A drugs, and when he was about eighteen the men who came to the house seemed more interested in Sofia than his mother. He wasn't sure when it started, but he noticed that his little sister started to have money. Then, when he arrived home one night, he caught one of her punters having sex with Sofia, whilst his mother sat in the same room, high on one thing or another. Chalky attacked the man and got a real beating for his efforts.

He pleaded with Sofia not to do it again, but the money was too great a temptation, and so it continued. Then, last year, at barely sixteen years of age, she had been introduced to someone who could find her plenty of punters, willing to pay a good price for abusing her young body. She was now working for a big agency in London, pretending that she was eighteen. Chalky told Daniel that she was beautiful, and that if he saw her he would be like every other man, and want to dick her himself. He hated yet still loved his mother, and continued trying to look after her.

He became involved with a gang stealing cars to order, for breaking or ringing, and got busted along with several others, after dropping off that night's stolen motor to a dodgy garage in East London. They hadn't been able to pin too much on him, but the judge still gave him five years. He calculated that, with time served, he would be out in another twenty-seven months.

After listening intently, Daniel then filled Chalky in with his own story.

Shortly after, Daniel was lying half asleep, when Chalky called out to him and said: "Bollocks are like dustbins: when they're full, if someone don't come and empty them, you have to take the crap to the tip yourself – so, don't worry if you hear strange noises."

Daniel smiled in the darkness and turned over, trying to ignore the slight rocking movements he could feel through the framework, and the muffled groans which followed. This was some cellmate, for sure.

10

ONE THING FOR certain was that Chalky could run. He often used his speed as his form of escape, twisting, ducking and diving away from his pursuers.

Daniel had a rugby ball and, along with a few others, used some of the free time to pass the ball around or, if enough of them, play a cross between rugby and American football – Tom Jenkins promised to try getting it recognized as an official sport. Daniel reckoned that, with his speed, Chalky could play pro rugby, and decided to nurture him. Although Daniel had chosen not to go pro, he still had a lot of contacts, and if Chalky turned out half useful he would get in touch. It might stop the kid wasting his life.

Johnny Greg and Paul Wilcox were both lifers, and had spent most of their lives in prison, for one thing or another. This time for Johnny it was armed robbery, and he was considered top dog in the prison. Paul was inside for having murdered his wife and her lover in an appalling manner. He had returned home after serving time for robbery with violence, and even though his wife had told him it was all over between them, halfway through his sentence he still had a key. He entered the house at night, found them asleep together and gagged and bound them at knifepoint. Paul then proceeded to cut off the boyfriend's penis and, whilst he lay there, bleeding profusely, raped his wife, before cutting both their throats. The boyfriend had been mixed race, and from that moment onward Paul had it in for anyone with colour in their skin.

Daniel got on well with everybody and, because of why he was in here, received a lot of respect from even the hardened inmates. But, Johnny had warned both Chalky and Daniel several times that if Chalky didn't bottle it up, he would not be responsible if Paul stepped out of line. Daniel himself had already intervened on numerous occasions, when Chalky's wit had gone too far, but it was not until Father's Day that things really exploded.

Chalky seemed to delight in winding Paul up, knowing that either Daniel or Johnny would calm him. Chalky had christened Paul as "Pussy" – when asked why, he replied that Paul was "Johnny's bit of pussy."

Many of the inmates had developed homosexual tendencies – especially the longer serving ones – and those who hadn't eyed any woman they came into contact with, perhaps more than many of them deserved. Bigger girls with nice faces, plain girls with nice legs or bottoms – all were acceptable, if they were birds in the hand. Some of the female staff were considered very attractive.

Daniel himself had been working hard on one particular officer, and would probably have got a lot closer, if he hadn't had to babysit Chalky. He suspected someone had guessed what was going on, or she had mentioned it to the wrong person, because suddenly she disappeared without any goodbye, and rumour had it that she had been transferred. Daniel couldn't ask, for fear of raising suspicions.

Besides, he was now just starting to work on another.

Father's Day had been a bitter day for Daniel, for years, but since he had become godfather to Sam and Victoria they sent him a Father's Day card every year; this year's had arrived at the prison that morning. Originally, Tina had written them for the children, along with his birthday and Christmas cards, a big kiss from herself and Tony, and a little kiss from each child. This year, though, Victoria had written the card by herself, and the whole thing was covered in kisses.

Father's Day was also a sore point for Paul. He had two children with his now dead wife, and had not heard a word from either of them since the murders. He was still convinced he had done them no wrong, and that what had happened was entirely their mother's fault. It was the wrong time of year to provoke him.

Regardless, though, Chalky taunted Paul again that day, regarding his sexuality, and how he must miss a real woman – that was, if he could ever get one. At recreation, Chalky continued barracking Paul as he played pool, with comments like "Nice shot, Pussy," or "Pussy's put one in the well."

The flashpoint came as Daniel and Chalky stood in line to be served their dinner; Paul and John were already sat eating theirs, at a table behind them. Chalky made some remark about the stew looking like cat food, when suddenly Daniel was aware of a sharp movement behind him and instinctively tried to block it, putting himself between Chalky and his assailant. Something flashed and a searing pain went through his shoulder.

All hell then seemed to break loose, whistles blowing and uniforms appearing from nowhere. Daniel was now bleeding profusely, and he was ushered away quickly. He could hear the others being ordered back to their cells as he left the dining area.

No sooner had he reached the sick bay, when another officer appeared and thrust something into Daniel's hand. The three officers then departed to return to the fray, if it had not already been quelled. As the doctor went to glove up, Daniel read the note:

"Say nought and I will see that your boy doesn't get hurt."

Daniel had no intention of grassing anyway. He knew full well that Paul had tried to blade Chalky. Luckily, the sharp object, whatever it had been, caused only a superficial wound, as it had caught Daniel in a sideward thrust when he pushed the arm away from Chalky's back; once it entered his shoulder, it hit bone and glanced across, rather than going in deeper.

Tom Jenkins appeared as Daniel was being stitched up. No weapon had been found and no one was saying anything. What he couldn't understand was that he knew Daniel had no enemies, yet Daniel was pretending to know nothing. He left muttering something about "honour amongst thieves".

Daniel was given the secure, single-bedded room in the sick bay – not because they wanted the option of locking him in, so Daniel was informed, but because it had the best mattress. The doctor quipped that he was on his own because there was a big football match on the television that evening, and no one wanted to be in the sickbay where there wasn't one. The doctor took several blood samples and gave

Daniel another tetanus injection, even though Daniel assured him that he was up to date, before leaving him in the care of the night nurse.

She was aged about fifty, but good for her age, and the more Daniel undressed her with his eyes, the better she looked. From their conversation, Daniel ascertained that her name was Cindy.

At about the same time, the officer who was supposed to stay on watch in the sickbay changed, as well. He complained that it was a total waste of time sitting there for twelve hours, when they were short-staffed on the wings. Cindy told him to go, as she knew full well that he wanted to watch the football; she stated that she could always lock Daniel in, if need be. The officer used the internal phone to get permission for her suggestion, then left.

At about nine, Cindy made Daniel a drink and gave him a packet of chocolate biscuits, then she sat on the bed, chatting. She noticed that the dressing was fairly soiled with blood, and offered to change it. Once she had removed it, she bathed away the blood which had run down his chest.

The mere closeness of her, and the fact that he could see some of her bra and breast through the gap in her uniform, turned him on. He implored her to wash lower down. Cindy just smiled and told him that he was a naughty boy. Still, Daniel got the impression that she enjoyed rubbing his muscular chest and arms, and asked her again, to which she this time replied that she would think about it.

Daniel heard her answer the midnight check-in and assure them that she was fine. Daniel was asleep, she said, and she would get her own head down for an hour or so herself. That she did – in Daniel's bed.

After the first time, Daniel asked her if she did that with all of her patients. She replied that he was the first, but then he was not a normal patient. She went on to tell him that her husband was now a big, fat, useless lump, who only had time for the bookies, darts, football and beer; she had needs, too! She admitted that his muscular torso had awoken her desires.

Her desire lasted all night, with brief interludes to check or be checked in. The last session had been particularly passionate, and his stitches had been ripped out. Daniel persuaded her to leave things as they were, and to tell the day shift that he had tossed and turned all night.

When the doctor arrived back on duty in the morning, he accepted the explanation and restitched the wound. He also gave Daniel something to help him sleep and placed the arm in a sling, to limit movement.

Daniel was devastated that three more inmates made their way into the sickbay that day, all with minor ailments which didn't require hospitalization – but, because the symptoms could have been real, it was safer to admit them. Cindy wasn't too pleased either; she had looked forward to a second helping before Daniel was returned to the wing. She did, however, manage to slip in when the rest appeared asleep, and partake in some heavy petting, which ended with her finishing him off by hand underneath the sheets. Her parting words to Daniel, before she went off shift, were to get sick again soon.

Daniel spent two more days in the sickbay, but even in his wildest dreams he would not have looked twice at the nurse who replaced Cindy on the night shift. He considered himself lucky that all had happened when it did.

Back on the wing, things returned to normal, and Chalky was apologetic and quiet. He realized that he or Daniel could have been killed, and with Johnny's help, a truce was called between Chalky and Paul. Paul had little to lose by killing Chalky – he would probably die in jail, anyway – but he didn't want to leave his comfort zone with Johnny.

The prison service obviously had other ideas, however, and although they never mentioned the incident to Paul, they just arrived one morning, about a month later, gave him ten minutes to pack and loaded him in a prison van. It was several weeks before the inmates heard he had been sent to a cat-B prison in Oxfordshire.

The summer didn't go too badly. The weather was good and, with his outside job, Daniel managed to acquire a healthy tan. Daily workouts in the gym or his cell kept his body toned. As Tom had promised, rugby was also approved as a sport.

Richard sent him pictures of all the heifer calves born and heifers calving in for the first time, as well as any other animal he thought Daniel might be interested in. This included the new litter of pups, individually photographed, for Daniel to choose from; he asked

Alice to do that for him. Copies of the accounts were also sent in monthly.

The architects loved his plans for Bluebell Woods, and had now put in official plans to the council for three-hundred homes, varying from two to five bedrooms each, on a 999-year lease. The whole area would be gated, and the stream dammed for a fishing lake; a golf course, two play parks for children, tennis courts and a clubhouse would all be included. The areas between the houses would be retained and maintained as woodland still, and the staff needed to maintain and service the estate would be self-financing from a yearly service charge. The architects had already unofficially been told it would be passed, and tenders had already gone out to perspective building firms.

In a blow, though, in late September, Daniel was told that his appeal would not be heard for approximately another eighteen months, which put the dampers on things for a while.

But, with rugby now on the curriculum, Daniel started to get a team trained up and wrote to local clubs, trying to persuade them to give them a game; Daniel's old club was to be their first organized match. There were a few ex-players among his recruits, notably two ex-forces players – one a prop and the other a wing forward. The second fellow was about 6'7" and eighteen stone – a real formidable brute.

Chalky was by far the fastest player, and he certainly wasn't lacking in guts. The first time he tried to tackle the big man, he found himself still moving forward, even though he had wrapped his arms around the guy's legs – he soon learned to ankle tap or hit him hard, low down.

Daniel realized that he had lost a yard or two on his speed by smoking, but with the long time he had to spend in his cell, it gave him some comfort. One of the warders brought Daniel in a couple of electronic cigarettes, which Daniel found satisfactory. Chalky doubled up in laughter when he saw Daniel puffing away on it. His quirky remark this time was something along the lines of, "Electronic cigarettes must be like having sex with a blow-up doll: a poor substitute, but cheaper than the real thing."

Daniel had by now clocked up his first year in jail. He hadn't found it too hard, except for his lack of freedom and female company, private space and choice of whom he associated with. He wasn't counting the days like some did; he had the appeal to get over with first, then he could start counting down the years.

The autumn and winter proved a success for the rugby. The first match against Daniel's old team went well, with the prison side winning by a 28-point margin, which definitely surprised both sides. Chalky ran in four tries and was certainly impressive. Most of the other teams were a bit skeptical; knowing rugby to already be a dirty game, they expected to be playing thugs, but Daniel had coached them well, and didn't dwell too long on teaching the finer points of the game. Word got around, and teams were soon asking for a match or a replay. That season, the worst they did was to draw twice, and one of those games was against the second team from a top professional club, which Daniel still had contact with. The other was a police side and, to be honest, it was the dirtiest team they had played against, with players sent off from both sides.

Whether it was the attention the rugby was getting, or just luck, both Daniel and Chalky ended up with single occupancy of double cells, side by side, and more often than not left unlocked.

Jimmy Tobin was sentenced to twenty years and his son twelve, for the arson and attempted murder of Tina and the children. Tina's insurance company was pursuing a claim for criminal damages which, if successful, would mean the Tobin farm being auctioned to pay for the damages. Richard had already acquired another estate nearby, of over 2,000 acres, and was primed to keep an eye on the Tobin property, and buy when it came up for sale.

Alice did manage a visit, and informed Daniel that the plans had been passed for Tina's house to be rebuilt, and that work had already started, with just a few material alterations from the original.

This was also the time that H.M.P. decided that he needed to start his rehabilitation.

Daniel's problem was that he had never admitted what he did was wrong; to H.M.P., this was the first step toward rehabilitation. The person allocated to achieve this was a young woman of about Daniel's age, named Rachael Moore.

Daniel's first impressions were of a miserable, dowdy and unattractive woman. He didn't exactly endear himself to her on the initial meeting, telling her he was not sorry for what he had done.

He was sorry that a man had died, but not because it was a direct consequence of what he had done; rather, because he had intended his victim to suffer for a long time. He knew it wasn't a nice thing to say – particularly for someone brought up the way he had been – but in this instance it was the truth, and he had always been brought up to "tell the truth and shame the Devil."

As these meetings continued, she gradually relaxed in his presence, and an occasional smile would materialize. They discussed what Daniel missed the most, and in return she opened up a little, and told Daniel that before their first meeting she had just ended a nine-year relationship. Daniel actually began to look forward to the meetings, not because he fancied her to any great degree, but because she was an interesting and intelligent person to be around.

She gradually revealed more of her personal life. She was an only child, whose father had died when she was young. Her mother had never really got over the loss, and had herself passed on, the previous year. Over a few months, she started to improve her appearance, and her attire along with it; soon, Daniel began to look on her as an available female.

Because Daniel was trusted to behave, unless a member of staff specifically wanted a prison officer present, he would be left with that official alone. She seemed to often bring up Daniel's sexual frustration, as if she enjoyed seeing him in such a state. She was fully aware that, apart from losing his freedom and his love of the farm, his other immediate and constant desire was a woman to fulfil his basic sexual needs.

Their next meeting had been set for mid-February, and Daniel was annoyed when the meeting was postponed for two days, so looking forward to it had he been. When the day came, and he entered the room, Rachael was already there. Daniel could smell that she was wearing perfume on, which was unusual, as it was considered inappropriate around the inmates. She was wearing a long, flowing skirt.

As soon as she had heard Daniel's escort go away, she rose and sat on the spare table in the corner, behind the door, and beckoned Daniel over. She had then hitched up her skirt, revealing she wore nothing underneath.

Daniel didn't need asking; he just took the opportunity.

He had taken himself in hand the night before, so was able to give a reasonable account of himself. It was lucky that the escort had gone away for a coffee, or he would have heard the sounds of two people climaxing noisily.

The same occurred the following month, on Daniel's 30th birthday, and again in May, by which time he was rather making love, than simply satisfying an urgent need – often managing twice within the allocated appointment time.

Then, the following month, he was shocked to find that he had a new personal officer. When he asked where Rachael was, he was told she had left. This new one was prettier, but an ice maiden; after two meetings, Daniel refused to see her again.

So, it was back to pleasuring himself. Unfortunately, the only other time Daniel had cause to go to the prison doctor was after a leg wound requiring stitches, suffered during a rugby match. But Cindy had not been on duty.

11

THE NEWS OF Jimmy Tobin's death filtered through the prison grapevine. He had been a member of a group brewing illegal alcohol. The last batch had been extremely potent, and several had ended up in hospital. Jimmy's liver was already in a bad state from his years of alcohol abuse, and did not recover from the latest binge.

Chalky and Daniel often had visitors at the same session and eventually Daniel met Sofia. Chalky was right: every man in the room would have loved to have her in their bed.

They were usually given adjacent tables and enjoyed some light-hearted banter. Chalky would tease Daniel that he never had any decent women in to see him, so that Chalky could, in his words, have a gander. In fact, Daniel had been working on getting another female officer to satisfy his needs, to which he thought Chalky might have cottoned on. So, just to shut him up, he sent a V.O. to Jennifer, Julie and Grace.

The look on Chalky's face when they walked in was priceless, and between them they flirted so much that Chalky was speechless. When Daniel told him that he'd had all three in one night, he shook his head in disbelief, but back in his cell started to sing something about having beautiful dreams tonight.

After a visit a few weeks later, Chalky told Daniel that Sofia had told him she worked with a girl called Candy, who knew Daniel. But, as all the girls used false names, Daniel was none the wiser, and any guessing would be pointless; he had never knowingly slept with a prostitute. If he had done so, he had never been asked to pay.

About a month later, Daniel got a message to ring David.

David explained that a certain Sophie Tobin had been in contact, and wanted to meet him. He advised Daniel that, having spoken briefly with her, he considered it would be to Daniel's advantage to listen to what she had to say; it might be helpful at his appeal.

Daniel agreed; he was intrigued as to what Sophie Tobin could know to help him. A visit was arranged, and she arrived with David the following week. She had definitely changed, though was still recognizable – and she was certainly a head-turner.

Sophie started off by saying that she bore no ill feeling toward him regarding her brother. In fact, she venomously snarled, he deserved it. Sophie then went on to tell how, when she had left home with her younger sister, she was pregnant. She wasn't sure who exactly the father was, but it was either her own father or Tommy.

The abuse had started before her mother died, when she was just twelve years old. She had been left to keep an eye on a calving cow, when her mother had gone to town. Her useless father had already gone out drinking, and Tommy and her cousin Cam were out on Cam's bike. They returned shortly after her mother had left; she found them outside in the yard, when she went into the barn to look for eggs.

She started to climb down off of the bales, when she realized that the boys were behind her. Cam made some suggestive remark about her showing a nice piece of thigh, then grabbed her and threw her down onto the loose straw, instructing Tommy to grip her arms. So, with Tommy holding her, Cam had raped her. Then the boys had changed places.

After that, she made a great effort to avoid being alone with them, but they waylaid her on several occasions. When Cam was killed in the police chase, she thought it would stop, but Tommy continued on his own, on several occasions. When her mother died, he was even more persistent, and once her drunken father and elder brother were both in prison, she had no defence against him.

When her father was released and returned home, he went straight out drinking, but seemed in a good humour. Tommy had tried it on again with her earlier, but on this occasion she grabbed a pair of scissors and he backed off, heading out himself.

When he returned home, she decided to tell her father, thinking that he would be outraged. Instead, he just grabbed her dress, ripped it from her and, forcing her back onto the settee, raped her himself.

After that it became a regular occurrence, with sometimes both of them on the same day, though she did not think that Tommy knew their father was doing it as well. Shortly after that, she realized that she was pregnant. Worse, she was becoming conscious that Tommy was increasingly casting his evil eye on their younger sister, now nearly thirteen.

Her father had asked a local dealer to give him a price on some store bullocks, but had then not been at home when he came. So, Sophie bartered a little with him, then accepted his offer. He wanted to take four of them on with him now, as they suited an order he had to fulfil; he paid Sophie in cash, saying that he would be back for the other fifteen the following day.

As soon as she had helped the dealer load the four steers, she showered, packed any worthwhile clothes of hers and her sister's, along with some trinkets and her savings, including the dealer's cash. She waited until her sister came home from school, and the two of them left.

She caught the bus to Salisbury, and from there the train to London, where she soon realized that the money she had would not go a very long way. They spent the first two nights in a bedpan hotel, and explained as much as she dared to her sister, who then admitted that Tommy had groped her and fondled her maturing breasts on several occasions, as well as slipping his hand up her skirt – she was glad to be away from there.

On the second night, Sophie slipped down to the bar to get them both a Coke. Although not yet sixteen, she looked older. Whilst waiting to be served, a man asked her if she was looking for business. Being naïve, she did not understand what he meant, and asked him what he thought she wanted. He laughed and told her.

She kicked him between the legs and left without the Coke.

Lying in bed that night, she considered what he had said. She came to the conclusion that, as she was not yet showing yet, if men were prepared to pay for it, then why not? It was a way of earning money.

The girls moved to a slightly better hotel, near the motorway, where Sophie explained to her sister what she intended to do. Then, she dressed herself up to look as sexy as she could, within the bounds of decency, and went to the bar.

She attracted attention immediately, and within half an hour found herself in someone's bed. Half an hour later she left with fifty pounds in her purse. Had the man asked her how much she wanted, she would have said just ten pounds; luckily for her, he had just handed it over, as if he knew the going rate.

An hour later she was back in another room. This time the man tried to barter the price beforehand, but she stayed firm and even demanded the money upfront. She saw five men on that first evening, before returning to her own room.

She continued this for four nights, before being rumbled by the hotel. She only lasted as long as she had because seeing her with a younger girl had thrown the staff off the scent.

At least she had learnt something from the experience; she booked into another cheap hotel, though in close proximity to several better class ones, in which she had plied her trade.

By the time she was seven months pregnant, she was finding it harder to get clients, and it was also very uncomfortable for her, should they get rough.

She found a small flat to rent, and eventually stopped work altogether, at about eight months. She had enough money saved to see them all through for several months, and for her younger sister to look after the baby when she started back to work. At first, all went to plan.

She gave birth to a little boy who, despite his parentage, appeared perfectly normal.

She had given herself three months off before starting back at work, and during that time often took her meals at a nearby café. There, she found herself attracted to a young man named Keith; although she was aware that he was a bit of a "Jack the lad", she eventually agreed to a date.

He always seemed to have plenty of cash, but when she asked him where he got his money from, he always replied simply that he did "a bit of this and that". After a few dates with him, she went back to his house and had sex with him. He wanted her and her sister to move in with him, and eventually she agreed.

Everything was fine for about a year, then his moods started to change, and he started staying out at night. After a bad row one evening, he went back out again, but this time left a drawer he usually locked open, with the key in the lock. She looked inside, and was horrified at what she saw: syringes and needles littered the bottom of the drawer. When he returned home, he admitted that he was using heroin, and had been for about six months. Sophie threatened to leave him, and would have done so, if she'd had somewhere else to go.

He gradually began to use more and more, and was often out of it for days on end. Sophie started working again, leaving her sister to look after the baby. Keith had also started to get violent, meaning that sometimes she was unfit to work. Eventually his expenditure exceeded his income, and because he spent so much of his time stoned, he hardly ever seemed capable of doing anything. It wasn't long before people were knocking on the door for money – not all for unpaid bills, but mostly for money he owed his supplier. He was now using more than he was selling, often leaving him in deficit regarding payment. Finally, Keith told her that she would have to go out and earn some money, and he even suggested her going on the game.

He had no knowledge of her past, so she pretended to protest, but this only resulted in her getting a beating. She called an agency, and was taken on immediately.

She always kept some of her earnings back, because Keith would take it all for drugs, leaving nothing for food. If Keith suspected she had kept money from him, he would beat her until she turned more over.

One day Keith went out, and that was the last time she saw him alive. He and a friend were found dead, having injected a bad batch.

But she was still living in the same house, working for the same agency and enjoying her life. It was here, as Candy, that she met Chalky's sister Sofia, when they were both sent to the same hotel. The radio was on in the taxi, reporting on Daniel's sentencing, and she mentioned that she knew him.

It was then only by the chance that the two women met again, just a few weeks ago, as Sofia had long since moved to another agency; but, once again, they had been sent to the same hotel. This time, they decided to take a drink in the bar, before leaving on their way to their next jobs. Sofia remembered Sophie telling her that she knew Daniel, and told her about her seeing him in prison.

Sophie went away and considered Daniel. She decided that if her experiences would be of any use in his appeal, she would like to help.

Daniel was touched by her story and, although he didn't say it, he wished that she had told someone what happened to her when it first occurred. He thanked her profusely, and suggested that she should come again, with Sofia.

David was certain her involvement would help, simply because it darkened significantly the character the prosecution had strived to make out to be such a good citizen, who wouldn't hurt a fly, rather than a persistent rapist – even of his own underage sister.

Daniel found himself slowly accepting the prison regime more and more, and could now only look forward to his appeal sometime next year. The upcoming rugby season brightened up the foul autumn weather, and they were allowed to use the facilities inside when the ground outside became saturated.

Several new inmates joined in as well, making team selection harder; in fact, Daniel occasionally left himself out of the starting line-up, or subbed himself off when the game seemed to be at their mercy. Several of the pro clubs had accepted pre-season friendlies, which gave Chalky a chance to show off his skills to some influential managers. Those who had played them before started to put out stronger line-ups, which even included some ex- and current internationals. Daniel was delighted at the amount of interest shown; he was certain that Chalky would be found a slot with one of them – especially when he outpaced and outmanoeuvred their best players to score (including a well-known English international winger, whom Chalky had caught and taken down within a yard or so of the line, preventing him from scoring).

Two of the other new signings were also worth of pro rugby: Dave Manning, a young Irishman, had been tipped for international stardom as a centre, before finding himself on the slippery slope, which had led to his incarceration for embezzlement; and Neil James, who apparently had the driving skills of a Formula One driver – except that he had honed his skills on public roads. For a big guy he had tremendous speed, and mouths would gape when they saw a prop keeping pace with centres and some wingers, for fifty yards. Daniel included both Neil and David, along with Chalky, in the sevens competition he organized, and they had run riot, keeping a clean sheet all the way to the final. Everything seemed to come easy for Chalky; he never seemed to put too much effort into anything, as though it all came naturally. Daniel supposed that this was in fact so.

With the rugby making such a good impression, a football team was also formed, and again it was surprising to see the standard of some of the inmates. Some had played for professional sides, and had even had trials for Premier League clubs. Daniel could not help wondering how so many talented men ended up in here.

Daniel himself was working on one of the female warders: a tasty, young, married woman, whose husband was also a warder at a nearby young offenders' institution. He'd had a quick snog or two with her, and fondled her body during more intimate moments, but she seemed loath to progress beyond the teasing stage. The whole thing might have satisfied her ego, but it certainly wasn't doing more than frustrate Daniel. What made it worse was that Chalky had seen her slip into Daniel's cell, and would not believe that nothing was going on. Daniel had needed to threaten him into silence in company – though that didn't stop him making snide remarks when they were alone.

Richard's visits were regular and welcome; on rare occasions Alice would accompany him. Tina was still staying with her, as even though her home was finished, she hadn't yet found the courage to move back in. It was obvious that Alice enjoyed her company, although she said very little about Tina or the children unless prompted, so Daniel let it ride without complaint. Tina hadn't asked for another visiting order, and Alice hadn't mentioned it. Daniel still felt bitter, and only out of a sense of duty to the children did he continue to send them cards at Christmas and their birthdays. In return, they wrote their little letters back to him, with the normal news of school, etc. Tina's Christmas card arrived early the next

December, as if to remind Daniel that he had still time to send her one.

January brought a shock.

Daniel rarely read letters, even though he still received dozens every month, with offers of sex and marriage – often with explicit photos enclosed. Daniel generally scanned then ignored them all, though he did share some of the contents with some of his fellow inmates. Not all were from the U.K., but it was an Australian stamp which prompted him to open one first from his latest batch. There was no return address, just a date.

The farther he read through the letter, the more shocked he became, growing increasingly sad and angry at the same time. The letter was from Rachael:

"Australia.

Dear Daniel,

This will come as a shock to you, and I am truly sorry for both deceiving and using you. You may have thought that our little liaisons were for your benefit, whilst in truth I was using you. I have thought long and hard about writing to you, but decided that you had the right to an explanation of why I left without telling you.

You may remember that I told you I had just broken up

from a long-term relationship when we first met. Well, my relationship was with a woman; yes, I was and still am a lesbian. When my mother died I decided that, as there was nothing to keep me in the U.K., I would start a new life in Australia, as this was where my father came from, and he always told me it was a better country to live in. I removed what I wanted from my mother's house and put it on the market, along with my own apartment. But, although I am a lesbian, I still wanted to have a child, and decided that you would make an ideal sire. Yes, a "sire", not a "father" – that is the real reason for our little moments of lust, which I must admit I actually enjoyed. I would advise that you should always take precautions during any meaningless relationship, as although I worked out my most fertile time of the month, I was caught first time! I did it for myself twice more, just to ensure that I had gone past the three months before I burnt my bridges. I did intend to come back once more, for your sake, but my mother's house sold quickly, and the couple who bought my apartment were in a hurry to complete, so I had to bring my departure forward.

I have a new partner now – yes, a woman. We went through a civil ceremony just over a month ago. We have opened our own business and are very happy. Please do not try to find me as you will be wasting your time. Australia's a very big country and my name has now changed. We have all we need.

The baby was born two weeks ago – a boy. I have named him after you. The picture I enclose is the only one you will ever get, but be sure that he will know he had a really good father. My sincere apologies for any deceit or hurt this may cause you.

I sincerely hope all goes well for you in the future. Hope prison isn't being too unkind to you. For all you have done for me I thank you, and will never forget, even though you were unaware of my wickedness.

Love, Rachael.

x"

Daniel picked up the photo, which had landed face down on the floor, and saw his son – his firstborn child – for the first and probably the only time: a chubby baby, lying asleep on a blanket. He had lots of hair, and Daniel could see a resemblance to pictures of himself as a baby.

His hand was shaking and he felt a tear trickle down his cheek. He was choked, but he knew that Rachael was right: he had to forget. Daniel paused for a moment, before tearing the letter into shreds. After taking a last look at the picture, he did the same with that.

12

CHALKY WAS ALMOST due for release. He had turned down the move to a cat-D for the last few months some time ago, and Daniel had arranged for Richard to furnish a cottage on the estate for him, as well as to find him some work. Chalky also had definite offers for trials at several clubs.

But, when the day came for him to leave, one would have thought he was the one being left behind. Privately, he hugged Daniel and cried, sobbing so much that Daniel had to change his shirt before leaving the cell. Chalky could not thank Daniel enough, and promised that he would make the most of his opportunity, and never let him down.

Daniel had to suppress the emotions he himself felt: pleasure at being able to help this young fellow, as well as regret that he was not the one leaving this place. There were still four months until Daniel's appeal hearing and, despite what David had said, he was still very uncertain of the outcome.

With Chalky vacating his cell, yet another recent convert to rugby was moved in, which now meant that the whole team were on the same wing. Daniel was well aware that this was a little more than a coincidence.

During breakfast, a few weeks after Chalky's release, Daniel heard some jovial remarks about a "dirty old judge" in the papers; when he went back to his cell and picked up his daily, staring right back at him from the front page was his very own Judge Jeffreys.

"JUDGE'S KINKY SEX ENDS IN GIRL'S DEATH" read the headline.

It appeared that Jeffreys had a liking for masochistic sex, which had gone too far, resulting in the death of a prostitute. Jeffreys had been arrested at the scene and charged with manslaughter. The following day, the story took up the best part of five pages, with other women coming forward with tales of his brutal treatment toward them - including the prices they had charged for the abuse.

Another article went on to talk about his life and career. Apparently, he was the only son of the late Sir and Dame Jeffreys.

Daniel's thoughts went to his own situation. He supposed that in a lot of ways he was glad that his parents couldn't see him like this – but at least, to an extent, his intentions had been honourable. Jeffreys must have been glad that his parents weren't still alive to read this rubbish.

The article went on to provide more of the family history, and apparently the lineage did in fact go back to the original Judge Jeffreys. Another small article mentioned the fact that some of the decisions Jeffreys had made, and the sentencing he had passed down, were now in question – especially where violence toward women had been involved – and a slew of appeals would undoubtedly be forthcoming.

David and Richard were both aware of the arrest when he spoke to them later. David warned Daniel not to put too much weight on that being the full answer to his appeal, though concluded that it would certainly help.

Richard and Chalky returned for a later visit, and were both very optimistic of Daniel's chances. Chalky loved the farm work and fresh country air, and Richard reckoned he was born to it. He also had a rugby trial lined up for Bath. He was profusely thankful for the car Richard had provided for him to get around. He had visited his mother in London, and was pleased to discover that she had been to rehab, and appeared to be staying clean for the moment.

He also informed Daniel that Sofia had been writing to Irish Dave Manning, and was planning a visit. He asked Daniel not to let on that she was still working as a prostitute, as he hoped that she would quit once he was released; hopefully he could provide for her.

Chalky came on his own the following week, full of news. It transpired that the cottage Richard had put Chalky up in was in fact the old Tobin farmhouse. Whilst in London, he had met up with Sophie; she had since visited her former home and planned to do so again. Daniel had the suspicion that things were a little bit cosier between Chalky and Sophie than he was letting on.

He then revealed that he had been offered a contract with Bath, but before signing he was concerned that he would not be able to do much farm work, once he started training. Daniel reassured him that this was not a problem; he could always pay rent instead of labour. Daniel had only said it in jest, but Chalky could not have been happier with the fact that he could still live there, at any cost.

Daniel still received regular reports from Simon, but even though it was making Daniel a very rich man, he had little interest in the business. Although Simon always came to him for the final word on any major decision, it was just a formality; he himself had a very wise head and years in the business, and Daniel knew that he could trust the man's intuition and loyalty, just as his father had done.

However, what transpired over the following week meant that Simon would play the biggest role in Daniel's early release.

To Daniel and David, aside from the character Judge Jeffreys being a judge and now a murderer, his past meant little to them. But the name had meant a lot more to Simon, for his own reasons – about which, once he was certain, he contacted David with his findings. A few days after the horrendous killing had hit the headlines, Daniel was informed that David had requested an urgent solicitor's visit. The prison staff had obliged, as always, and it was a beaming David who arrived an hour later.

Jeffreys's father had apparently got involved with a scheme, some 28 years earlier, for which he had borrowed a large sum of money from Daniel's father. The scheme had turned out to be a total failure, with Jeffreys senior taking the biggest loss. Unable to repay his debt, he had been forced to sell the family home, which had been in the family for hundreds of years. Rather than blame himself and his fellow cronies for their bad judgement, he had chosen to blame Daniel's father for the loss of the family estate, and had often been heard to slate him maliciously. It had now become obvious that Judge Jeffreys had been aware of this animosity; he must have rubbed his hands with glee when he found the son of his family's arch enemy in the dock before him. Daniel hadn't stood a chance at a fair trial.

David had already lodged an appeal for Daniel's immediate release on this basis, and had also gone to the press with his findings. Calls for Daniel's release came from all quarters, including his local M.P., and websites and petitions were set up on the internet.

Daniel had a gut feeling that, with all the publicity, his appeal would be successful. In fact, things moved far quicker than anyone had expected, or even dared hope for.

Daniel was sat in his cell, when Tom Jenkins knocked and entered. If he was aware that the door was not locked, he didn't say anything. He simply put his arm around Daniel's shoulder and informed him that he was being released on licence the following morning. He lent Daniel his personal mobile phone to ring Richard, and request that someone was there to pick him up. Daniel was shaking as he did so, still not really sure what was happening.

When Tom left, Daniel noticed a small bag had been left on the bottom bunk. Inside it were a half-bottle of Jack Daniel's and a packet of cigarettes, along with a note reading: *"Your favourite tipple, I believe. Use for medicinal purposes only."*

Even though it was late evening, word soon spread around the prison, and shouts of congratulation could be heard late into the night. Daniel hardly slept a wink, even with Jack as company, and was up early, to pack his possessions into the bags and boxes provided.

He donated most of his belongings to his fellow inmates, and when he went for breakfast found that he couldn't eat a thing. The atmosphere in the canteen that morning was unforgettable: slaps on the back were so regular that Daniel had to ensure nobody was within distance every time he tried to snatch a drink from his cups of coffee. There were handshakes all round from fellow inmates and staff.

Daniel was given the clothes he had arrived in, to change back into before being escorted to the reception area, to collect his possessions and await his lift. Having given away so much, he had only two bags and a box to take out. He had to wait for a while, as several inmates on R.O.T.L.s were checked out, before, once again, handshakes and good wishes were forthcoming and numerous.

Finally, Daniel was allowed outside, to stand once again a free man.

Even though it was the same sky that he had seen as he walked across the yard to the reception, out here it seemed clearer; the sun seemed warmer; the birds seemed to sing louder; and, now free, the roses he had nurtured in the gardens seemed more fragrant.

Daniel smoked a real cigarette from the packet Tom had given him. Nothing was pretend today; this was for real.

13

RICHARD WAS A Volvo man, so when a convertible Audi with blacked-out windows pulled up in the car park, Daniel barely gave it a second glance. Instead, he walked to the nearest flowerbed, and bent to take in the full fragrance of the peace roses, already full in flower.

He lifted his head as the Audi's driver door opened and a shapely pair of high-heeled legs swung out – this was enough to catch his immediate interest. It was a shock when the head appeared, and he realized that the legs were Tina's.

She called out to him: "Looking for a lift somewhere, stranger?"

Daniel picked up his belongings and made his way to the car, throwing them into the already opened boot. He straightened up and took a good look at Tina. "You look good," he managed to blurt out, somewhat annoyed that it was she who had come to fetch him.

"You don't look bad yourself," she replied.

In the next second, her arms were around his neck and she was crying. Daniel put his arms around her and stroked her hair, as she buried her head into his chest. "You smell good, as well," Daniel commented, as he took in the seductive odour of her perfume.

"You bought it for my birthday, four years ago," she sobbed.

Daniel remembered. He had asked Tony what she liked and

bought it without even smelling it. Still, he mused, he probably would have done anyway, if he hadn't liked it. It was no wonder that the prison didn't like female warders wearing perfume whilst on duty; it was immediately arousing.

Tina explained that Richard had an important meeting that morning, so she had offered to do the honours. She had also felt obliged to collect him as she was still living at his house with the kids and Alice. She had not been able to face going back into her own home, blaming it on her decision to have it rebuilt identical to the original. She had obtained planning permission to build a bungalow, and this was now nearly complete. But, if Daniel wanted her to, she would find somewhere else before its finish.

Now free, his bitterness seemed to be subsiding, and he assured her that whenever suited her would be fine, and that, in fact, her being there with Alice had been good in some ways, as he had seen that Alice was ageing, and needed someone to take the load off of her.

Tina offered to let Daniel drive, but he declined, telling her to just stop at a pub on the way home, where he could get a pint and a proper English breakfast.

Daniel reclined the seat a little and adjusted his leg room, sinking back in the soft, leather upholstery. Free of the prison at last, he could now relax and enjoy the fleeting countryside and its smells. Freshly mown grass, left behind and baking in the sun, leaving that sweet odour, made one hungry; even the smell of slurry spread on aftermaths was enticing to his nose. Although pungent at times, it was still more pleasant than the latrine odour which always seemed to hang around the cells, whatever anyone did to try sweetening the place up. Not much was spoken, Daniel enjoying the openness, which stretched in places without an obvious end, and the country smells that drifted through the partly open window.

At times, Tina's perfume seemed stronger. That, and sly glances at the thighs which were more exposed, now that her skirt had worked its way higher when she was seated, aroused Daniel. He promised himself it would not be too long before he would enjoy running his hands over something similar, even if his charm had waned and he was required to pay someone like Sofia for the privilege. It had been a long time since Rachael, and he had no time for teasers. Tina must have seen his sly glances, and probably read his thoughts; when they had to stop at traffic lights, she tried to discreetly pull her skirt down.

A pub was found before too long and, with the sun now warming quickly, they were able to sit outside and enjoy an unhurried, nicely cooked breakfast. Daniel swallowed his first pint at the bar without stopping, feeling the ale flow sweetly down his throat. The second he sipped with more caution, as Old Tom was an extremely potent ale, and he could already feel the effects of the first on a nearly empty stomach. Tina and Daniel chatted about all sorts – kids, schools, cows, prison life and local gossip, as well as his chances on appeal – without touching too much on either's personal lives, past or present, to any great degree.

Returning to the car, Tina lowered the hood, tied a headscarf around her long, flowing locks and fished out a pair of sunglasses from the centre console.

With Daniel now unable to see her eyes clearly, some of Tina's remarks were more pointed and personal, which he tried to defuse by answering abstractly. They were now on the A35 and Daniel could smell the sea.

Alone in his thoughts, he glimpsed a bunch of balloons billowing in the breeze, tied to a telegraph pole. There was a placard underneath, which he could not read, so quickly were they past it, and so deep in thought had he been. It reminded him of his journey to court, on his last day of freedom, and the well-wishes posted along the route. Shortly after that he saw another bunch and, taking greater interest, saw that these had been placed to welcome him home.

"News travels fast," he commented, speaking aloud that which was meant for his own consideration only.

Tina told Daniel that a party for his homecoming was being arranged, as they travelled by his old rugby mates and the local community. Daniel wasn't sure that the terms of his release allowed him to do as he wished but, as Tina explained, they didn't want him in prison, and certainly wouldn't be looking for some silly excuse to send him back.

Landmarks were now very familiar, with little change that he could see, and he was eagerly anticipating Tina's movement to indicate their turn off of the main road, and head for the village and home. Balloons, ribbons and placards were everywhere now, and when he saw locals stood outside their homes, businesses and the pub shouting, waving and blowing him kisses, he became wet-eyed. Tina told him that they had expected his arrival time an hour earlier, as she hadn't anticipated he would want to stop for breakfast. Daniel would have to apologize for keeping them waiting, but was deeply touched by their actions and patience.

Tony had been among these people for the majority of his life, and Daniel was not too vain to believe that their forgiveness and acceptance of what he had done was just because they liked him; he knew it was mainly because of their love for Tony, and, to some degree, Tina – not to mention their dislike of the Tobin sons and their father.

They left the village behind and were now passing the Tobins' old home. Richard had done an excellent job of having the place renovated and, apart from all he could see appearing a well-kept and managed unit, Daniel could not help noticing the blaze of colour which generated from the flowerbeds, from the farmhouse gate toward the house; he nodded in approval at Chalky's obvious efforts and pride in his home. Tina's new bungalow still had work vehicles on a definitely unfinished drive, and Daniel was surprised to see it being built so close to the road, but made no comment.

Within a few seconds, Tina had slowed and turned left across the cattle grid at the bottom of his drive. Again, the lawns were well manicured and flowers abundant, even at this time of year. The only noticeable difference was the size and spread of the Pampas grasses, which waved their elegant plumes of pink and white from several locations around the garden, as if they too were welcoming him back.

The front tradesman's entrance was open, allowing the freshness of the outside to enter and brighten the large room which served as a changing room, when one came in from work – a freezer room and general store also among its many uses. One door led off to the kitchen and another to the back stairs, which Daniel had trod countless times when he came in late, or more often arose before dawn, without disturbing the rest of the house. One had to be up early to beat Alice, as she was out by six a.m. most days.

The dogs must have recognized the car and ignored it, but Alice had heard it too, and softly said to Jessie that her master had arrived. Jessie immediately jumped from her basket beside the AGA, and no sooner had Daniel left the car than she hurled herself, whimpering, into his outstretched arms. The sound of his voice brought the other dogs out, two of them barking. Seeing the affection others were bestowing on Daniel, they all joined in, vying for the attention Daniel was trying to share between them.

Daniel then looked up and could see the large, roly-poly figure of Alice stood in the doorway, already wiping away the tears which trickled down her cheeks, so happy was she to see him. Beside her leg and the door jamb a small, curly-raven-haired head peeped out, trying to comprehend the reason for the commotion around her, while little Timmy pushed past them and jumped on a pedal tractor, totally uninterested in his or his mother's arrival. Still keeping an arm dropped, so that Jessie and the others could lick it whenever they could manoeuvre themselves in a position to do so, Daniel quickly made his way to Alice and, as big as she was, he lifted her up in his arms and hugged her to himself. Daniel could feel the wetness of her tears as they flowed profusely, and the heaving of her body as the sobbing wracked her. Daniel dropped her back onto her feet but did not release her from the embrace, tears now flowing from his eyes, as well. How long their embrace went on, Daniel was not sure.

When they eventually untwined, Daniel looked down at the timid little girl beside her and asked: "Who's this?"

The only answer both women offered was that her name was Donnanita. She was certainly a beautiful little girl, her hair so curly it fell in ringlets, and her face unforgettable, with those deep-brown, innocent eyes, which looked at him questioningly. Daniel ruffled her luxuriant curls and gave her a wink. Donnanita rewarded him with a shy smile.

Daniel wanted to change and shower and, after a cup of Alice's full-milk coffee and one of her Senior Service cigarettes, went to rid the last of the prison reminders from his body. Jessie accompanied him, as of old, and even had the audacity to lie on the bed without an invite, as she waited for him to finish.

Daniel returned to the kitchen, where a large slice of Alice's homemade lardy cake was waiting for him. Having been informed that lunch would be an hour, Daniel rejected the offer of a second slice.

Little Timmy was now playing with a farm set, using the dog baskets as fields. He answered when spoken to, but was intent on doing his own thing. Daniel tried to make friends with Donnanita, but the little girl was apprehensive of him. Tina informed him that she didn't see too many men, and it took her a while to trust them. But she had endeared herself to Chalky, and loved stroking his luxuriant, black hair, which shone like silk.

Halfway through his second cup of coffee, a loud knock came at the kitchen door, followed by the immediate appearance of the man himself.

Chalky embraced Daniel tightly, before picking up the child, who had now attached herself to his leg. Although Chalky normally spoke in a typical cockney accent, Daniel had heard him mimic the tongue of his forefathers many times, and it was in this way that he spoke to the child, who soon became a giggling, laughing being. Chalky stayed for only a few minutes, with the promise of seeing Daniel later that evening.

Donnanita became more talkative when she realized that Daniel was a good friend of Chalky's, and before long was sat upon Daniel's lap, stroking his grade-2 prison cut. Daniel teased that she would be a hairdresser when she grew up, with her liking of hair. During general conversation, Daniel ascertained that she was two years old, and had been born on his own birthday – and, she was very much Tina's child. Daniel did some quick reckoning, and came to the conclusion that her father must be the C.I.D. friend of Tina's, who had been hanging about so much around that time. Daniel was a little shocked by this fact, but who was he to judge? Unless everyone had clammed up on him, Tina had clearly not pursued this relationship – perhaps because he was a married man.

Alice had prepared one of his favourites: homemade faggots, wrapped in the apron from one of his own pigs. The promise of roast beef for tea was almost enough to make Daniel shudder; he'd already eaten twice as much as he normally ate in a full day, but at least his tastebuds had not suffered – and he was certainly enjoying being spoilt.

After lunch, Tina took Timmy and Donnanita upstairs for a nap, volunteering to take Daniel around the estate when they were asleep. Daniel did not really want to meet too many of his workforce, and because of this Tina kept away from areas where they would run into them. Even though, some were close enough to recognize the Range Rover, and waved or flashed their tractor lights in welcome, suspecting the second occupant in the vehicle was Daniel. She stuck as often as possible to high ground, where they had views which covered large areas of the estate.

Satisfied, and having other things on his mind, Daniel got Tina to drop him at the farmhouse gate. He whistled once and the dogs came down, at full pelt. Sam and Victoria would be home from school by now, but Daniel had something he wanted to do first, before he saw them. He vaulted the gate he'd had to open the last time he went through it, more than two-and-a-half years earlier, and strode out briskly toward the oaks, which still stood proud against the sky.

Reaching them, he was pleased to see that the area had been well maintained; even the seats had been recently varnished. The trees were now just about at their best time of year, verdant and fresh.

Daniel reread the inscription engraved around the seat – not that he had forgotten a single word, or the horror of the day they commemorated, which now seemed like a lifetime ago.

"Well, Dad, I've managed to survive the lion's den. With a bit of luck, I'll never have to go there again," Daniel said out loud, as if expecting or hoping for a reply.

He sat down on the same seat he had done on his last day of freedom, and tried to evaluate his present situation. He really needed to find himself a decent woman and produce an heir. Even these stately oaks made sure that they left behind their successors, to keep the line going. Daniel just hoped that his parents, were they looking down on him now, would consider that he hadn't disgraced the family name.

Jessie had taken up position at Daniel's feet, and as he mused and smoked one of the cigarettes given to him the previous evening, she could be heard to occasionally sigh as she slept, her head resting on his feet. Alice told him that the dog had taken herself off to his bedroom every night, and cuddled into the old clothes he had left her. She was certain that Jessie had understood her, when told that it was her master back in the car, because she had leapt from her basket and rushed to the door, while the others had hardly raised their heads at the sound. Since then, she hadn't been a yard from his side, and had even waited for him to be seated before relieving herself.

Daniel rose and made his way back down to the house. He would return soon to share some private thoughts, but the living were waiting for him, and he had so much going through his head at that moment, it was not the right one for peaceful meditation.

Sam and Victoria were waiting for him in the garden, and nearly crushed him with their vigorous embraces. Daniel apologized for not having any presents for them, but promised to take them shopping at the weekend. At least they hadn't forgotten him; it was genuine affection they showed. With one holding each hand, they went inside for dinner.

Alice had done them all proud; the dinner would have been fit for a king. When it was over, Tina sent Sam and Victoria to have their showers, and took little Donnanita off to prepare her for bed, before getting ready herself. Alice bathed little Timmy.

Daniel spent a while in the garden, before Alice came out and cuddled into his shoulder, enjoying the early evening calm and each other's company again. Birds sang sweetly as they flittered amongst the branches of the fruit trees, catching the multitude of tiny insects which seemed more abundant at this time of day. She had been like his mother for years now, and although she may not have agreed with everything he had done, she never wavered in her love for him, or ever criticized him, even in private. Daniel loved the old lady. He would have to get someone in to do her job, or at least help her, as it was about time that she took things easier. Tina might have been good company for her, but again tonight she was going to babysit, while they partied. It was probably only a one-off, and he knew Alice wouldn't have come, anyway. He would have to find another way to treat her – perhaps a holiday.

Alice chided him to go inside and get ready for his welcoming party, all of which would probably already be at the rugby club, half-drunk. Richard was not back from London yet, but Jen had promised they would be there later.

Daniel completed his preparation within a few minutes, then took out the pile of correspondence he had brought back with him from prison. He opened the bag containing cards, from the last three Christmases and birthdays. Taking out the ones from Tina, he studied them closely. The first Christmas card had one big kiss, three medium-sized ones and a tiny one, as did his birthday card. The others all had one big and four medium-sized kisses: one from each of them. When Tony was alive, there had always been two big and three medium sized.

Tina appeared in the kitchen, just as Daniel finished his second double whisky. She looked stunning in a short, red dress, and Daniel couldn't help but compare her to the eighteen-year-old malt he had just drunk; she got better with age, for sure. She again volunteered to drive, with Daniel insisting that she take the Range Rover, in case his ability to hold his liquor had diminished after over two years of forced abstinence; at her frown, he explained that he didn't want to spoil the interior of her new car, should this occur.

On the short journey to the rugby club, Daniel enquired whether her boyfriend would be coming, and she said that she didn't have one. When Daniel asked about Donnanita's father, she just replied that the child was the result of a one-night stand, and she hadn't told him, because he wasn't around when the baby was born. Nor was she proud of what she had done, asking others not to tell him, as she felt ashamed. When Daniel pressed her over whether he knew the father, she replied that he did, but she would not be telling him. Daniel continued, suggesting the C.I.D. officer. At this, she repeated more angrily that she was not going to tell him, adding that the officer he referred to was married; just what kind of person did he think she was?! Daniel knew he had touched a nerve, and was immediately sorry for what he had said.

Her manner was still chilly when they arrived at the rugby club, where pennants, balloons and banners billowed from every available anchoring point, even the top of the rugby posts. A large crowd was outside drinking, as they waited for his arrival, and as soon as they realized it was Daniel arriving, a massive cheer went up.

Back slapping, handshakes, hugs and kisses were the norm for the next half an hour. Drinks from several different spirit bottles were thrust into his hand, which he obligingly drank. Several were keen to tell him that his release had made the national news that evening. Daniel hadn't seen it, as no one had found the need to watch television, with him just home. Most of the village and all of his workers turned up to wish him well, and Daniel put several hundred pounds behind the bar for drinks. Most had one or two before returning home, but the support for him was more than obvious, and Daniel was extremely touched.

Daniel, not now used to drinking, was slowly becoming inebriated, and when the buffet food was put out, Tina slipped off to get two platefuls, making sure she picked up plenty of bread for him. While she was away Richard and Jen arrived, and made their way to the table where Daniel was holding court. On seeing them approach, Daniel rose and hugged his two friends. Richard placed two bottles of champagne on the table and went off to find some glasses.

With most of the group now disappearing to find food, Daniel was able to have a few minutes alone with Jen. The subject of Donnanita came up, and Jen apologized for keeping him in the dark, explaining that it had been Tina's wish; she had been sure that Daniel would not be pleased, being such good friends with Tony, and having ended up in prison, trying to prevent him ever learning of the rape. She went on to say that it was lucky the baby had survived, being born nearly two months premature.

Even with his brain not working at its sharpest, now that the alcohol was taking effect, her words put a new thought into his head, and he tried to redo his calculation of earlier.

Tina arrived back with two plates; the one she offered him would not have held another cocktail sausage. Daniel thanked her and tucked in, the alcohol enhancing his appetite. Tina's plate held very little, although she did fancy a little more of something which had appeased her palate, and went to get it.

Richard came back, accompanied by a different Jennifer – one with whom Daniel had been *very* acquainted in the past. She pointed out her new partner, talking to some villagers on the other side of the room, and told him that, as much as she wouldn't mind a rerun of the last time, they were here together, so it was a definitely a non-starter. Then, after a quick kiss and a hug, Jennifer went back to the middle-aged man she had indicated was now her partner.

Richard explained that she had met him while working, and he had chased after her for several weeks, before she agreed to date him. He was obviously a lot older, but a rich widower, which had probably been the initial deciding factor in her decision; now, however, she seemed genuinely very happy with him. He was obviously unaware of her wanton past, but Jennifer probably felt secure with him; most of the village males had been with her at least once, and she had always seemed to have a nose for ferreting out any female indiscretions.

By the time Tina returned with her replenished plate, several other women had gathered around Daniel and Richard, with two of known ill repute sitting on each side of him. Daniel started to rise immediately, to give her a seat. She shook her head and pushed him back into the settee, before promptly sitting on his lap – as if laying claim to his attentions. This didn't go unnoticed by Richard and, meeting Daniel's eyes, he lifted his eyebrows and smiled.

Tina's closeness was almost too much to bear; he could feel the erection which now strained to rise even harder, against the restraints of his trousers and her body weight. Although she showed no signs of awareness, he was certain that she must be, and that the reason she shifted her weight on several occasions was not because she was uncomfortable, but to tease him more. Daniel could smell her and feel the soft warmth generating from their bodily contact, which only increased his desire. He made the excuse of needing the toilet, to escape his embarrassment.

Two of his old teammates were in there, and the ensuing

conversation made him forget the fairer sex for a while, as they discussed Chalky, and Daniel's own possible return the following season.

Having relieved himself, Daniel considered going outside for a bit of peace and quiet, but he knew there would still be a lot out there, on such a nice evening as this. He was beginning to feel a little pressured, with so many people around him after over two years away from it all. So, instead he went into one of the cubicles, put down the lid, pulled out a cigarette and sat down on the seat.

Jen's words came back to him: *nearly two months early; a one-night stand, Tina had said.* Working back from his birthday to the day Tony had been buried would fit in with the other facts, and could well make Donnanita his. Thinking about it, the child had the same colour hair and his, which also went wavy as it grew longer. He had to find out.

Daniel returned to the lounge, where another pint was waiting for him, as well as glasses of champagne poured. Richard stood and made the toast to him, then Daniel thanked them all for standing by him, and invited everyone to a barbecue at the farm, the following Saturday evening.

Someone grabbed his arm then, as the disco started again, and he found himself with several partners for the next twenty minutes, dancing to some good old hits. Daniel took a breather and another drink, before returning to the dancefloor. The dancing, if a little frenzied at times, nullified the effects of the alcohol, and Daniel began to enjoy himself. Tina had a spell before crying off, saying that her feet hurt too much to continue – but made him promise the last dance or two with her. As the evening progressed, the music slowed down, as did the dancers, until it was announced that the disco would be ending in fifteen minutes, then the bar half an hour after that. Several tried to claim Daniel for a dance, but he insisted that he had already promised Tina.

Daniel offered his hand to Tina and pulled her from her seat, still holding her as he led her to the floor. The D.J. played "Brothers in Arms", one of Daniel's favourites. Daniel and Tina started at a respectable distance, but as the song continued, they eventually ended up with their bodies pressed together. It felt good, and it felt right. As Daniel pulled her closer, Tina responded by tightening her grip on him, and moving her hips so they were even closer. Daniel stroked her hair before gently kissing her head, now nestled on his shoulder. Gentle as it had been, Tina must have felt it, because she responded by nuzzling his neck.

Daniel pulled back, and enquired of Tina that, if he asked her one question, would she give him a truthful answer. She nodded. Daniel then lifted her head, so that he could look directly into her eyes, and asked her if he was Donnanita's father.

Tina just nodded and pulled herself close to Daniel, before whispering in his ear that she had been too ashamed to tell him. She didn't want to put any pressure on him. Then, once he had grown bitter toward her, when he went to prison, there was no way that could she tell him.

Daniel asked her if Alice knew. Again she nodded, telling him that Alice was the only person she had confided in; everyone else had been told Tony donated semen to a bank, once they knew that he was ill; even if cured he may have been infertile. People had been told that the baby was the result of a third attempt at conceiving, as he had wished.

Daniel shuffled Tina toward the D.J. and, once close enough to speak, asked him to play Boris Gardiner's "I Want to Wake Up With You" as the last song. The song currently playing was "Lady in Red", again appropriate, with Tina wearing red.

Daniel guided her to the side of the stage farthest from the bar, with less lighting, before tilting her head back and finding her lips. The kiss was long and passionate, lasting almost as long as the remainder of that song, and the one he had requested.

When it had finished, taking Tina by the hand, Daniel led her back toward the D.J. Using the mike, he thanked all again for coming and for putting on the party for him, reminding them of the invite for Saturday night. Tina then recovered her handbag and, with a swift goodbye, they left, hand in hand.

The farmhouse was in virtual darkness when they arrived home. Once inside the house, they kissed again.

When they broke, Daniel led her to the back stairs, saying: "No one-night stands this time."

They kissed passionately, the moment they reached his room, their lips barely parting as they tore each other's clothes off. Then, with hands and mouths rampantly seeking and caressing the most intimate parts, Tina pulled Daniel back toward the bed. As soon as they reached a horizontal position, he entered her with his rampant member. Their lust was shortlived, but the climax was earth-moving.

They lay together, still united, panting from their urgent explorations, before Tina spoke; she said she had been dreaming of this. Daniel did not reply, but the gentle nuzzling and kissing indicated that he, too, was of the same opinion.

Lovemaking this time was passionate but gentle, and once it was over, they fell asleep in each other's arms, still coupled. They were satisfied for now – and content that they had once again found one another.

14

THE MORNING BROUGHT a different scene inside and outside the house.

Alice was singing to herself as she prepared the breakfast, and gave a knowing smile as Daniel and Tina appeared, hand in hand. Tina whispered in Alice's ear, but Daniel's keen sense of hearing confirmed that she had told her he knew about Donnanita.

With the national news having announced his release, the press and T.V. crews were in the lane in their hordes, hoping for an exclusive interview at best, or glimpse long enough for a picture or two at least. Tina took one look and gave up any idea of taking Sam and Victoria to school. As soon as anyone appeared at the door, cameras flashed. And the phone rang, incessantly.

In the end, Daniel phoned Chalky and asked him to creep in the back way. All known callers would show on the phone face, so Chalky was asked to answer any unknown numbers in his black tongue and "coon talk", as he called it. Chalky was very inventive, and Daniel and Tina nearly split their sides laughing at some of the rubbish he came out with.

When the paparazzi were still there in the afternoon, Daniel loaded two cartridges into a shotgun and made his way to a side-bedroom window. He slowly pushed the barrel of the gun through the curtains, just over the top of the open window. When he saw a pair of pigeons flying overhead, he pulled the trigger twice. The gun was aimed high in the sky, but Daniel calculated that at that angle the spent pellets would rain down harmlessly on the waiting reporters.

It worked: within a few minutes, most of the reporters had left, although the incident was mentioned on the evening news. This prompted a reply from local police, stating that, as the shots had apparently been fired at a greater distance than fifty yards from the public highway, and with no intent to harm, there had been no laws broken; as far as they were concerned, it was the end of the matter. The statement did, however, follow a call from the local constabulary, to enquire if the shooter was a registered licence holder, and if the shots were fired at legitimate targets – which, in light of the news, explained their enquiry.

Daniel spent the late afternoon playing with the children, before the excellent meal Alice had prepared. Chalky, Richard, Jen and the family, along with David, joined them for a private celebration, and discussion of the present situation. David was certain that, with the new revelations, Daniel would be released permanently considering time served.

After dinner, they retired to the lounge and a few drinks, whilst Tina put the children to bed. As promised, Daniel read both Sam and Victoria a story, when they appeared from the bathroom.

Halfway through her story, Victoria enquired if he was now going to be their father. After she had answered his question of whether she would like him to be, by throwing her arms around his neck and kissing him numerous times, Daniel replied that he would, if it was what her mother wanted. Victoria tried hard to convince him, with sloppy kisses and hugs, that she did, to which Daniel promised her that if that were so, then he would love to be her new father. She kissed him again and immediately fell to sleep, a smile apparent on her face.

Sam was not quite so direct, but indicated his wish to stay at Daniel's home indirectly, by telling him that his bed here was nicer than the one he had slept in at home, and that he loved Alice's breakfasts. He too then fell asleep, listening to the *Thomas the Tank Engine* story he had chosen for Daniel to read.

Timmy and Donnanita were fast asleep by the time he reached their rooms, and Daniel smiled to himself as he watched Alice moving toys off of Timmy's bed, before safely tucking him in. Daniel watched Donnanita for a few minutes, before gently kissing the sleeping child, taking in the fragrance of her recently shampooed hair and powdered body.

When Daniel returned downstairs, Richard and Jen had gone home to get their own little ones to bed, leaving a message that they would return tomorrow. David left soon after and Chalky about two hours later.

When Tina insisted that she would do supper, Daniel was left alone with Alice. He crossed the room and placed his arm around her, to which she responded by laying her head on his shoulder and taking his other hand in hers. Daniel kissed the now nearly white hair and, placing a finger on her lips, told her how much he loved her. He then asked her how she would feel about taking a back seat, and his asking Tina to marry him.

She replied that she thought Tina was right for him, but thought he preferred her cooking. Daniel laughingly assured her that there was no way he was demoting her, but that he just wanted her to have an easier life, as any cared for mother should. A few tears were shed by both, and they embraced as if mother and son.

Tina appeared with the supper: port, a cheeseboard and coffees, which were enjoyed by all.

An hour later, Daniel insisted that he do the washing up – though he cheated, by putting it all in the dishwasher. He let the dogs out for their final toilet, wiping their feet on their return, and promised them a good walk in the morning. Jessie made her way to the back stairs, while the others returned to the warmth of the AGA, displacing the cats who had quickly taken the place in their absence. The cats were Tina and Victoria's, and true farm cats, earning their living around the farm by catching vermin; they were supplemented with waste milk, and leftover cooked rabbits Daniel shot. He had also noted several cases of cat food, and guessed that Alice preferred to feed them this in his absence.

Daniel retired and saw that Jessie had already taken up her usual place, in the basket between his bed and the radiator. Tina was combing her hair in front of the wardrobe mirror. Daniel gave her a light kiss on the back of her neck as he passed, noting the skimpy negligee she was wearing and feeling an instant erection.

As he showered, he realized that he would need a more feminine outlook to furnishing their boudoir, if she agreed to become a permanent part of his life.

The fact that she had returned to his bed tonight, rather than retire to her own room, was a good omen. Tony had said she was highly sexed, but she assured Daniel that Tony was the only other man she had been to bed with. As soon as he got into bed beside her, she started kissing, nibbling and licking him, gradually working her way down his body, until every inch of him yearned for her.

For such a slight woman, she was immensely strong, resisting his efforts to avail himself of her body, with crafty movements of her arms or crossing of her legs, which aroused him further. At last, she made herself available, increasing the nibbling of his neck and ears to an extent that, had he not been in the throes of passion, he would have considered it painful. Her leg was wrapped around his, her body moving as if they were already coupled; Daniel could feel her wetness on his leg. God, she was more than hot. Their lips met, and it was as if she wanted to devour him, so hard did she kiss him, biting his lips from time to time.

She manoeuvred him onto his back and, without using her hands, lowered herself onto him, teasing her clit with the rampant penis, before letting it enter her. Holding his hands down beside his head, she dictated the pace, taking him to the brink on several occasions, before slowing the rhythm or stopping completely for a short while, until she could feel the pulsing of his member abate, before slowly increasing the tempo again. Although not that big busted, in Daniel's mind her breasts were just perfect: firm, with nipples now swollen with desire. From time to time, she would bring them within Daniel's reach before pulling back, as he tried to prevent her, by sinking his teeth in hard around their swollen mass.

He shut his eyes, begging for completion, and for a split-second he saw Liz, grinding herself on his mouth, while another had ridden him behind her. He shook the memory away.

He could feel Tina's juices engulfing his testicles, as she increased the voracity and speed of each thrust. The murmur from her throat was increasing in volume and pitch, until it almost became a scream. Daniel himself could stand no more and, freeing one hand, grasped her buttock, trying to pull her yet closer to him. Together they climaxed, with such noise that Daniel heard Jessie jump from her basket and momentarily place her feet up on the bed to investigate the commotion, before returning to her basket, satisfied that he was in no danger.

Tina collapsed upon him, their lips meeting for a long and sensuous kiss, both still breathing rapidly. The bed was now more akin to a swamp, as the sheets soaked up not only the sweat from their bodies, but also their joint body fluids, now slowly seeping from Tina, as his erection subsided. They stayed like that for several minutes, as their breathing and heart rates returned to normal, now content with just the closeness of each other.

At last, Daniel spoke: "Victoria would like me to become her new dad. Do you think that would be a good idea?"

Tina did not speak, but Daniel could feel the affirmative movement of her head, as she still rested on his chest. Her lips once again found his.

Daniel awoke early the following morning, feeling a little cramped. Tina still slept soundly, sprawled upon his body, and even as he tried to slide out from beneath her, she stirred and tried to regain her position on him. When free of her, Daniel kissed her gently and left the bed.

He had a busy day, and wanted to take the dogs for a good run before breakfast. Daniel showered and quietly dressed, before quietly leaving the room with Jessie, and made his way to the kitchen. For once, he had risen before Alice; looking at the kitchen clock, he could see why: it was barely five a.m.

He shared some plain biscuits with the dogs, as he dunked several of his own in a mug of sweet tea, before setting out for his favourite place.

He noted that even the younger dogs had learnt to negotiate the cattle grid, and only Jessie waited, as always, for the wicker gate to be opened. Daniel was reminded of the last time he had taken this early morning pilgrimage, but being earlier in the year, the air was warming with the morning sun, foliage was more verdant, birds more vocal and, when he glanced up toward the oaks, he could still see a lot of wood, their leaves not fully out. He smiled smugly to himself as he vaulted the gate, as if he had been doing so regularly, rather than for the second time in two-and-a-half years.

Rabbits scurried away in abundance, their white tails showing their disgust at being interrupted. Their population had obviously increased a great deal during Daniel's absence, and would afford him some good sport. Instead of the three musketeers breaking cover, Daniel could see a red doe nervously pacing below a patch of gorse where, if Daniel was correct, her fawn was concealed. She was well aware of the danger posed by the dogs, should they approach. They probably would have done, but for the sheep netting and three strands of barbed wire preventing them access to the field, as she was clearly visible to them. She would then have taunted them into giving chase, at the same time leading them away from her fawn. Thinking of the strength of the maternal bond reminded him of his own mother, and in some ways Alice, who had taken it upon herself to become his surrogate mother.

Daniel was glad he had kept fit; the hill was steep, but he reached the gateway to his sanctuary without any noticeable increase in his respiratory rate.

He was more aware of the surroundings than two days ago, and was instantly aware that somebody had spent considerable time tending the area, and revarnished the seats. This time he walked around the huge trunks twice: first to read fully the verse he had written – even though every word was already imprinted clearly on his mind – and second to observe the scenery before him. It was a beautiful day, and Daniel was pleased to see that little had changed.

There was a new barn at Richard's, and a new roof could be seen on the Tobins' old farmhouse, along with new sheeting on the original Dutch barn. He could also see the new bungalow's roof, though its construction was hidden, being lower than Tony's old home, which was now rebuilt. The mature trees and gardens which surrounded it were still there, which made it look identical to the original, even new. A conservatory, erected only a few months before the fire, had been rebuilt and included in the restoration.

In the distance, Daniel could also see this year's lambs, calves and foals, grazing alongside their mothers. A hen pheasant, along with her brood, searched out the insects from a clump of nettles, not fifty yards away, whilst above him he could see a pair of grey squirrels scampering along the branches, and hear the rapid tapping of a woodpecker, as it pecked where a limb had broken off, some years before. Butterflies and bees settled on the flowers around him, both gathering nectar and fertilizing as they went. God, it was good to be alive and free.

Daniel sat down on the seat facing the rising sun, soaking up its warmth and breathing the slightly salty air, carried in from the sea. He reached into his pocket and opened the cigarette packet. He lit one and inhaled deeply, feeling the rush instantly. He knew he should give it up, or smoke the electronic ones, but seeing that his daily intake varied between two and ten smokes, he didn't chastise himself too hard – even though he knew his mother would be horrified.

Daniel glanced at the heavens, crossed himself and said: "Forgive me, Mother, if you are watching." Then, as an afterthought, he added: "You too, Dad. You will be pleased to see that the lions never ate me, and hopefully I'm a free man again. I promise to try never shaming your name again. Sorry."

At that very moment, a small Columbus cloud, which had partially shielded the full strength of the sun, slipped past, as if giving him a favourable sign from above. Daniel blew four kisses toward the sky and felt a tear trickle down his cheek, as he pictured their faces again in his mind. He tried to envisage how they would look today. He also imagined Ruth now. Daniel had received one venomous letter from her, shortly after his incarceration, but nothing since.

Reality returned and it hit Daniel hard. He had so much to do and a lot more that needed doing: a will to properly sort out, people to thank – and in some cases reward; a wedding to plan – engagement ring first, of course; barbecue to organize. Additionally, he planned to go around the estates today, including any new acquisitions, with Tina and Richard, answer bail, buy the kids something and have a meeting with his legal team. Perhaps it wasn't all that easy to be a free man, after all.

He sprang to his feet, whistled the dogs, and set off back to the house at a jog.

Both Alice and Tina were already up and in the kitchen. Tina was laying the table for breakfast, and he caught her from behind and playfully nibbled her neck, before giving her a light smack on her buttock. Then he released her and went over to Alice, who was cooking on the AGA, giving her a peck atop her head. "Hope this is not going to be a case of too many cooks spoiling the broth," he quipped.

"If you don't like it, go back to where you came from," Tina replied, with Alice laughing in agreement.

When Tina took the children to school, Daniel asked Alice if there was any way she could find out what Tina's ring size would be. She immediately left the kitchen and, on her return, stated simply: "M." Tina had brought a dress ring for the corresponding finger the previous year, and the box was still in her bedroom.

Tina shortly returned with the news that a local P.C. had been stationed at the end of the lane, and was refusing to let the press through. He had told Tina that his superiors were concerned after the incident yesterday, and were not sure that Daniel should be in possession of any firearms while on licence. They were not going to pursue the issue, but would rather prevent another situation in which questions might be asked.

Armed with this information, Daniel asked Chalky to take him out, under a blanket in the rear of the Range Rover, so he could carry out some of his tasks in peace. As they were leaving, David phoned and said that there was little point at this stage having a meeting, as little more would be accomplished in this time. Answering bail was treated as equally trivial, with the bail officer – another of Tony's old mates – telling him not to bother, unless he'd left the country!

So, toys for the children were next on the agenda, and this part was easy: a Sylvanian Families manor house and more characters for Victoria; a Scalextric set for Sam; a prebuilt farmyard with fields, for Timmy; and a Dior cuddly rabbit for Donnanita. He also picked out some gifts for Richard's children, which he hoped they would like.

Daniel then got Chalky to drive to Crewkerne, where he knew a jeweller he had used before, who kept some really nice pieces. He was more than delighted to have several trays of diamond rings to choose from, in the correct size, and selected one with three large, yellow stones of high clarity. Chalky also took a keen interest, asking the prices of several cheaper ones – which again fuelled Daniel's suspicions that things were a little more serious between him and Sophie.

When they returned to the farm, Richard was waiting for him. This time Richard, with Tina sat beside him, drove him out under a blanket. The local constable was still there, along with a horde of reporters.

Daniel instructed Richard to stop, and Tina said in a loud voice that she didn't know why they were hanging about, as Daniel had gone to visit his grandfather in Scotland. Apparently it worked, because they all soon disappeared, trying to find out where this "grandfather" lived.

Richard's latest acquisition was on the A303 at Mere: a 2,800-acre estate with two large dairy units and the rest arable. He had retained the previous staff and manager and, as the sale had been motivated by a break-up of a partnership – caused by one partner running off with the other's wife – had not had to make too many alterations to date, on a well-run estate. Daniel loved the vast, rolling area of cereals, and could see that the cattle already contained a good proportion of Holstein blood.

Tim the manager was a worker, which became quickly apparent

when Richard found him in the process of servicing a forage harvester. Daniel liked the firm grip of his oily handshake, for which he apologized profusely after realizing what he had done.

A short walk from the workshop to the lovely farmhouse, nestling hidden behind a stand of firs, saw an open door and a voice calling them to come in.

An hour going over up-to-date books and talking shop left Daniel well pleased with this purchase, and even though it became apparent that Tina had been here with Richard before, she, like Daniel, was full of praise for both Tim and Richard on the way home.

When they arrived home, Jen had picked up Victoria and Tom, along with her brood, and they were all happily playing in the garden. Alice had the barbecue out, and lit it as soon as she saw them coming down the lane. The dogs and children were all waiting as the Range Rover stopped, and it was bedlam as they all tried to get to Daniel, to thank him for presents, or for a friendly pat.

Little Donnanita stayed at the back, still clutching the rabbit – which he later learned she hadn't put down – until the throng dispersed to continue their playing (or, in the case of the dogs, to linger close to the smell of meat cooking on the barbecue), before coming over to Daniel. He crouched down to her level and gently took her arm. She pursed her lips and pushed her face forward, to give him a kiss. "Thank you," she said, then added: "but, can I have a real one?"

Daniel laughed and nodded, at which she ran to her mother to tell her the news. Tina looked at Daniel and shook her head, smiling.

"Sucker," she said.

After the barbecue, Richard and Jen took their leave, and Daniel helped put the others to bed. This time, he went to Donnanita's room first, and read her *Benjamin Bunny*.

Halfway through, her grasp on his hand relaxed. After reading another page, he slowly disengaged his hand from hers and turned to go.

Tina was standing silently in the doorway. "You will make a good dad," she said, puckering her mouth for a kiss, as her daughter had done earlier. "They are waiting for you to say goodnight."

Daniel spent a few minutes with each, before joining Alice and Tina in the garden. Tina opened a can of beer for him as he approached, before topping up hers and Alice's glasses with some rose wine.

Chalky had been to training and, on his return, Daniel left him chatting to the women, whilst he gave the dogs a short run. When he returned, the women went inside to make coffee and discuss the food requirements for Saturday night.

Chalky said that Sophie and Sofia were both coming down the next day, and that he was going to ask Sophie to marry him. Daniel was delighted, and the two of them went into the house to inform the women.

That night, as Tina sat brushing her hair, Daniel knelt beside her and asked: "Can we make this official?" He put the small box in view.

Tina nodded and opened the lid. She gasped at the ring, which

Daniel removed and put on her finger.

Lovemaking that night was tender and somewhat magical. The following morning, Daniel awoke to find Tina still entwined around his body.

Tina proudly showed off the ring at the breakfast table. Hugs and kisses from Alice and the children followed, though the joy and laughter was a little darkened, when Victoria said: "Well, now we've got a real daddy again."

Tina's visit to the village, later that morning, put her in a state of panic. Everybody had said that they were coming on Saturday night, and she couldn't see how they would cope. Daniel had already foreseen this and, after letting her and Alice panic for a while longer, informed them that a professional firm of caterers was coming in thirty minutes, to discuss the requirements.

When they arrived, Daniel left them to it, to make some discreet phone calls to arrange children's entertainment, a D.J. and fireworks, among other things. He also invited some who he thought would like to attend from outside the area.

He had offered an olive branch to Ruth, too, but the reply he received later that day left him in no doubt about her feelings.

Early the following morning, two large marquees were erected and portaloos placed in the adjacent field. With the weather set fair, the field became a beehive of activity, as various companies and individuals involved in the preparations set out their equipment.

Once everyone appeared to be happy with what they were doing and where, Daniel slipped off to meet David and one of his partners, to rewrite his will and attend to a few more impending issues.

Saturday morning arrived.

The sun shone down from a clear, blue sky and everyone appeared excited, and the children and dogs hyperactive. In fact, by two p.m. they had just about burnt themselves out, so Tina sent them inside for a nap, which was achieved by Daniel reading a book to Victoria, Sam and Timmy, whilst Donnanita fell asleep in his arms. Daniel placed her gently in her bed and, as he bent to kiss her head, she stirred and murmured: "I love you." Daniel wiped a tear away with the back of his hand, and made his way quietly from the room.

Outside, Tina and Alice had been joined by Chalky, Sophie and Sofia. Chalky appeared as hyper as the children had been, and when he told them that Sophie had agreed to marry him, it became obvious why. Sofia also told them that her Davy, as she called Irish Dave, had asked her if they could try living together when he was released.

Tina looked at Alice and said: "Your turn now."

Everyone laughed as Alice replied: "No chance; I like my own company in bed too much."

Even though the start time was scheduled for six, people started arriving at five.

By half past seven, Daniel surmised that everyone who was coming was now there, so he asked the D.J. for the use of his microphone for a few moments. He had taken Tina's hand, and she now stood beside him. He started off by thanking everyone for coming, and being so supportive to them both. He thanked his staff for their hard work and loyalty, and Alice for her unselfish and undying love. He then went on to tell all his staff, including those in Reading and London, that he would pay for a fortnight's holiday to anywhere in the world, for their whole families – as long as they didn't all go at the same time. He then announced officially his engagement to Tina, but joked that they wouldn't set a date yet, until after his appeal; he had no intention of getting wed in a prison chapel. He also joked that Chalky's holiday would probably be a honeymoon.

Several others grabbed the microphone, to say a word or two of well wishes, after which Daniel and Tina sought out several in the crowd for special treatment. Howard and Simon were given the papers he had drawn up with David, to make them partners in their respective firms. Richard and Jen were given the deeds for the farmhouse, and the thirty-odd acres on which Jen had so successfully built her "pick-your-own" business. David was given the keys to a brand-new Range Rover, which Daniel knew that he lusted after; the chairman of the local football club a letter, authorizing him to build a new clubhouse (as long as it was named after Tony); and lastly, but not least, Chalky was told that when he and Sophie married, the farm would be their wedding present. Of course, the rest of the evening went well.

Alice took the children off to bed at about nine-thirty, but the D.J. played until one a.m., when the party was officially finished for the forty or so remaining stragglers.

15

A month later, Daniel was told that his appeal was successful, without even appearing in court. Having viewed the evidence, the judges did not deem it necessary to do so. He was therefore a free man.

Having made front-page news yet again for a few days, the farm was besieged by reporters and television crews, but the only statement Daniel gave was that he wasn't giving one.

Later that day, Daniel and Tina walked to his favourite spot and sat silently for a while, hand in hand.

Tina broke the silence by announcing that she wanted to be buried here. Daniel agreed that he would like that too, as long as they were side by side.

Tina then brought up the question of their wedding date, and advised Daniel to make it snappy, as she thought she was pregnant again, and didn't want to walk down the aisle with a bulging belly.

Daniel was overjoyed, and they ended up making love beneath the rustling leaves.

The wedding was planned as quickly as possible.

Once again, Daniel tried to get Ruth to bury the hatchet, but again her reply was offensive, to say the least. Through the grapevine from Simon, Daniel heard that her marriage to a rich banker had failed, and that she was now living in little more than a squat, in Battersea.

On the day, Daniel had two best men: Richard and Chalky, the latter of whom was now a regular first-team player, and officially engaged to be married a month after Daniel. Alice was matron of honour, and Victoria and Donnanita bridesmaids, along with Jen and her two eldest daughters. Sam and Timmy were pageboys.

They honeymooned as a family, on a quiet island in the Maldives, and returned with just days to spare, for Chalky and Sophie's wedding. This time, Daniel was best man.

Daniel honoured his promise, and gave them the deeds for their farm at the reception.

Sofia was Sophie's chief bridesmaid, and with Irish Dave now out on licence, it looked as if they would be next to wed; intentionally or not, she had ended up with Sophie's bouquet.

EPILOGUE

SIX YEARS LATER, and an increase in family size twice over, life seemed good to all. Sophie had been told a few weeks prior that her brother was shortly to be released, but they didn't expect any trouble.

Late one dark evening, the doorbell rang and Tina answered it, to find no one there. When it rang again a few minutes later, Daniel went to answer. Again, no one seemed to be there.

He switched on the outside light and, telling the now barking dogs to be quiet and stay, he peered out into the darkness.

The last thing he saw was a flash, as from behind a bush, someone fired two buckshot rounds into his chest.

As his body fell backward, onto the floor, six black and tan shapes jumped over and around him before, snarling, they leapt into the darkness.

Even though it was later said they could hear her screams in the village, it was already over before Tina reached Daniel's prostrate body. An inquest later revealed that he was so badly torn apart, they had just put him straight into a sealed casket.

Tina heard a car shoot off at high speed, and watched the lights of the getaway vehicle, gathering speed as it went away. Then, she heard the crash. The driver had lost control and hit a parked material handler on its solid weights, before exploding into flames. D.N.A. later showed the driver to be Ruth. The shooter was James Tobin.

It was a huge, but extremely sombre crowd which braved the weather, to follow the horse-drawn carriage to the top of the hill, where they filled the first of the double plot, consecrated some years earlier, next to the spot where Daniel had buried Jessie, four years earlier. With the wind and rain, bare trees and no flowers, it seemed a bleak resting place, but Tina knew that, come spring, it would be alive with colour and birdsong – a place where she could sit, reflect and mourn.

In the spring, a simple headstone was placed on Daniel's grave. Its inscription read: *"As I waited for you, you must now wait for me."*

AUTHOR ACKNOWLEDGMENTS

I would like to thank thank LR Publications for giving unknown authors like myself the chance to get their work published. I would also like to thank those members of my family and friends who have encouraged me to get my books published.

Lastly I would like to thank my well behaved cows who gave me the opportunity in my isolation with them for long hours to develop my stories.

PUBLISHER
ACKNOWLEDGMENTS

The publishers and authors would like to thank Russell Spencer, Matt Vidler, Susan Woodard, Leonard West, Edward Winters, Lianne Bailey Woodward and Laura Jayne Humphrey for their work, without which this book would not have been possible.

ABOUT THE AUTHOR

Educated at Reading grammar school but instead of going on to university followed my heart and worked on the land.

I have always enjoyed writing poetry and short stories mainly for the younger members of my family and then later on novels.

In each of my stories there is some personal truth and various characters have given me inspiration to adapt or enlarge upon.

I enjoyed shooting and gardening in my spare time but now retired I spend considerable time in Spain.

ABOUT THE PUBLISHER

L.R. Price Publications is dedicated to publishing books by unknown authors.

We use a mixture of both traditional and modern publishing options to bring our authors' words to the wider world.

We print, publish, distribute and market books in a variety of formats including paper and hardback, electronic books, digital audio books and online.

If you are an author interested in getting your book published, or a book retailer interested in selling our books, please contact us.

www.lrpricepublications.com

L.R. Price Publications Ltd,
27 Old Gloucester Street,
London, WC1N 3AX.
020 3051 9572
publishing@lrprice.com